Those Summer Nights

an Oyster Bay novel

Olivia Miles

~ Rosewood Press ~

Also by Olivia Miles

The Oyster Bay Series
Feels Like Home
Along Came You
Maybe This Time
This Thing Called Love

The Misty Point Series
One Week to the Wedding
The Winter Wedding Plan

Sweeter in the City Series
Sweeter in the Summer
Sweeter Than Sunshine
No Sweeter Love
One Sweet Christmas

The Briar Creek Series
Mistletoe on Main Street
A Match Made on Main Street
Hope Springs on Main Street
Love Blooms on Main Street
Christmas Comes to Main Street

Harlequin Special Edition
'Twas the Week Before Christmas
Recipe for Romance

ISBN 978-0-9995284-4-0
THOSE SUMMER NIGHTS

First Edition: August 2018

Those Summer Nights

Nights

an Oyster Bay novel

Chapter One

The Lantern had been home to many special events over the years, happy to offer a dry roof, a view of the Atlantic, and fresh catch from its rocky shores. It had hosted birthdays, graduations, engagements, even, a few times, funeral receptions. Evie Donovan had stood on the sidelines for most of these events, solidifying her reputation as a wallflower, no doubt, when in fact, she merely considered herself an observer.

But today, she was the star of the show.

She should have known something was up when her father asked her to work an extra shift on Sunday, when she'd already told him, exactly two weeks earlier, that Saturday night would be her last night tending bar. Officially. The Lantern had been her father's restaurant forever. Of course, she would help out here and there, just as she always had, but this whole bartending gig had gone on long enough. All summer long, in fact. It was time to get back on track. Put her hard-earned degree to use. Hang up her apron.

Still, she never could say no to her father…And so, at five minutes to four, on the day before she was scheduled to start her *real* job, she pushed through the front door of the restaurant in her black skirt, tee, and flats, which was not a uniform but rather her personal preference, and let out a scream when two dozen people, their faces a blur, shot up and yelled "Bon Voyage!" all at once.

She might have screamed in surprise. But it felt more like horror. And the fact that she'd screamed at all was disturbing enough, filling her cheeks with heat and making her wish she could dart back out the door, rewind time and tell her father no, she was sorry, but she couldn't come in today. She didn't deserve this. She had merely bartended for a couple months, out of desperation, because despite her perfect grade point average all through high school, college, and grad school, and despite the part-time jobs that supported her studies and the clinical hours, too, she had failed to procure a position as a licensed therapist in the Boston hospital where she'd interviewed last spring. And she wasn't going on a voyage. She was simply going down the street. Downtown Oyster Bay was so small that if she stood on the restaurant's wooden deck, she could practically see the back half of the building that housed the *Gazette*, where she would start work first thing tomorrow morning as, well, an advice columnist.

Sometimes she wondered what her professors and mentors would have said about that. About any of it, really. They had high hopes for her. Hopes almost as high as she had for herself once. Pipe dreams, really. Ambitions that were out of reach, or perhaps maybe never within reach at all. She'd been overly confident, sure that if she did her part the universe would do its part in return. That if she made a plan, stuck to it, and never lost sight of her goals, that somehow she would reach them.

She would laugh over that someday. But not yet.

Oh, dear, she was being pulled in for a hug now. She laughed nervously, realizing it was just Eddie, her cousin Margo's husband. She locked eyes across the room with her father, who beamed with pride, and tossed her a wink. He was clearly thrilled with himself for pulling this off, and well, who was she to ruin his party?

So she smiled and accepted a glass of champagne that Joann, a lifer at The Lantern, was passing around. She'd stop at one drink, because she planned to go to bed at eight sharp tonight to be fresh for tomorrow. Her second chance. Her new start. Even if it was nothing at all like she'd planned.

Now her sister was approaching, her eyes wary, and she grabbed Evie's elbow and hissed, "Of course I knew about this but Dad insisted it be a surprise, and so I couldn't tell you. Please don't be mad."

Evie had been mad at Hannah for many things over the years, but all that was finally becoming a faded part of their past. "It's fine. He's happy. And this was nice. Really, totally unnecessary, but very, very nice."

Maybe her father would miss having her around. Or maybe this was his way of giving her permission to go, to venture beyond the lobster-shaped wall clock and the fisherman's netting décor that flanked the bar of this fine Maine establishment.

Or maybe she was analyzing things too much again. After all, she still lived at home, still slept in the twin-size bed with the pink quilt that was turning threadbare. Since she'd returned from Boston over the summer, she hadn't even bothered to unpack more than her clothes, and everything from her life there was now stored in the attic, next to the tangled Christmas tree lights and boxes of baby clothes and dusty remnants of other phases of her life that had come and gone. How much could her father miss her when she was in trouble half the time for draining the hot water tank before Chip had a chance to shower? And when it wasn't her, the other half of the time it was Hannah, whose life was nearly as big a mess as her own.

But not really. After all, Hannah had a job and a boyfriend and, well, hope for some semblance of a future outside her childhood home. Evie, on the other hand...

"Excited for tomorrow?" Hannah plucked a glass of champagne from the tray that Joann was eagerly thrusting at people and took a long sip.

Evie sighed. Over the years she'd wondered if she would ever be like her older sister. Confident, casual, breezy. Hannah took life in stride. She fell, she got back up. She took chances. When was the last time Evie had done any of those things?

Well. She took a small sip of her drink. There had been that...*thing* this summer. That...*fling*, one might call it. But it was over. He'd gone back to New York. She had stayed behind, pouring drinks, and reprimanding herself for even thinking about those nights down on the beach, with just a blanket, a basket of crackers and cheese and wine from the Corner Market, and...

"Evie, you can't leave me. Don't say it's true."

Evie turned and grinned as Ron approached. Her first unofficial patient. Evie had helped Ron through a messy breakup with his wife, who'd been shagging his buddy down at the docks, and she knew it was acceptable to give her notice once he announced that he had finally worked off his community service hours for slugging Jill's lover, and had taken up knitting, which was excellent for the nerves, and not unlike the knots he was so good at tying on his job on the docks.

Still, Ron had a long way to go. Three days ago, he'd successfully hacked into Jill's Facebook account after weeks of trying and publicly reinstated the status of their relationship. "We are technically still married," had been his excuse, and all Evie could do was frown in response, because he knew how she felt about that, and the way he hung his head a few minutes later confirmed it. Still, he couldn't quite hide his smile, and the thrill of victory in his voice when he'd announced his behavior was troubling.

"I'm still around, Ron. And I'm still a friend." She smiled and gritted her teeth only slightly when he pulled her in for a barrel hug. He smelled like beer and fish. She wiggled her nose.

"It's not the same," he said, tears watering his eyes as he finally released her.

Oh, Ron. She had a special place in her heart for Ron, and well, it felt good to be needed.

For a moment, she wondered if she was making the right decision. All her life, she'd had a plan. A simple one really. She would work hard, get good grades, and then she would have whichever job she chose. When she got to college, she scoffed at the usual age-appropriate activities like kegs and parties and coffee dates that went on all night, and instead kept one or two close friends whom she did sensible things with like going to the movies or out for a slice of pizza, but most of all she studied. She graduated at the top of her program, all while earning clinical hours. And then…she couldn't get a job!

She wasn't well rounded enough; at least, that was their excuse. Really, she wondered if it was the blonde hair. She wondered if they could see the armpit sweat stains that even the bathroom hand dryer couldn't make disappear, so great were her nerves in the minutes leading up to that interview. Everything she'd ever done had led to that moment.

And now she was going from bartender to Agony Aunt. Not part of the plan.

Perhaps sensing her self-doubt, her cousin Abby jumped in and said, "I think an advice column is just what this town needs. And who better to write one than Evie?"

"She sure does give the best advice I've ever heard," said Ron, nodding his head sagely. He sniffled, hard, and because Ron was known to shed his share of tears over these past few weeks, Evie now kept a box of tissues behind the bar.

She leaned over it and pulled one out. He blew his nose hard and gave her a brave smile. Aw, Ron. Despite his big, burly exterior he really was just a teddy bear.

"What am I supposed to do if I start…thinking about her again?"

Evie stifled a sigh. Jill and Dave were now living in bliss, the divorce papers had been filed, and Evie had encouraged Ron to keep his mind busy, but there was always the occasional blip in this plan, like the Internet stalking, the numerous attempts that Ron made to break into Jill's email account, and, of course, the sad time that he sat outside Dave's house all night staring into the windows, until Jill herself took pity on him and brought him a cup of coffee and a bag of his favorite cookies.

Evie grinned. "Write me a letter."

Ron didn't look very convinced. "Write you a letter?"

"Ask Evie. That's the name of my new column."

Hardly original, but heck, she'd never been one for cutesy.

"And you'll help?" Ron asked, uncertainly.

She patted his hand, releasing it quickly when she felt the soggy tissue press against her palm. "Always, Ron. Everything will work out fine."

And it would. For Ron…hopefully for her, too.

She pulled in a breath and released it slowly as she turned back to her sister, who was frowning at her in the most peculiar way. Of course, Hannah didn't approve of how much Evie interacted with some of the day drinkers at the restaurant. Most were summer tourists, in for the weekend, but others were just loners, looking for a little conversation. They needed an ear. And Evie…she needed to listen.

"You don't look very happy, and something tells me it's not because of the balloons."

Evie smiled. Only Hannah would know that Evie had a strange aversion to balloons because she hated the sound of them popping. That and the embarrassment she'd faced at one childhood birthday party, where they'd all been told to sit on their respective balloons until they popped, and Evie, being a rather thin child, couldn't seem to make hers pop. The misery had gone on for what felt like five hours, but what had probably only been five minutes, and she hadn't earned a prize.

These were the sorts of stories people told their therapist, she mused. The types of stories she'd been prepared to sit and listen to, except that she'd blown it by not joining enough clubs in school. There was always private practice, but Boston was full of them already and she questioned the demand in Oyster Bay. A town as small as this made people nervous about privacy. Something told her they'd be much more comfortable writing to her anonymously.

"I just hope that I'm doing the right thing. An advice column?" Evie looked at her sister skeptically.

"Hey, I was the one who suggested that job! And Sarah works there too," Hannah reminded her, and Evie felt momentarily ashamed. Hannah was now the photographer on staff at the paper, and she was grateful enough for the opportunity. And Sarah Preston, the newest member of town, had turned into a friend since Evie and Hannah had returned.

Evie craned her neck for her now. No doubt she was here, and no doubt she was scouting for men. As if someone new would show up. It was late September. All the summer people were gone.

Hannah softened her tone. "Look, it's not my dream job either, and God knows it's a far cry from my life at the magazine back in San Francisco, but it's low pressure, it's experience, and it's fun. And you deserve to have a little fun, Evie."

Evie had to admit that when she allowed herself to relax this summer she had indeed had quite a bit of fun. Still, she wasn't one who could ever be satisfied living her life by her whims. She was much too practical for that.

She'd come too far and invested too much and sacrificed…She'd sacrificed too much fun for all those years just to start having it now!

"It might be a good balance," she said hesitantly. This was the exact wording that Hannah had used when she'd come home from work two and a half weeks ago and pitched Evie the idea. She could help people, but just in a different way.

"Wasn't that what I told you?" Hannah asked with a grin.

"Yes, and it's true. You're a good sister," Evie said, meaning it. Not long ago she might not have been able to say those words. But they'd worked on their relationship, spent time together, resolved all those issues that had bridged them apart. Well, almost.

Hannah chewed at her lip now, and Evie felt a sense of dread. She knew that look. Hannah was thinking of something, something she wasn't sure she would say. And Evie wasn't so sure that she wanted to hear it.

The back of her neck started to tingle. *Please not a hive*, she prayed. She thought her days of her panic manifesting in a skin rash were behind her. But Evie knew, because she knew her sister, and because she knew the one sticking point that was still between them. Their other sister. Their half-sister. Kelly.

"I have something for you. I've been holding onto it…" Hannah reached into her bag and pulled out an envelope. Neat and crisp. A simple white envelope by the naked eye, but to Evie, it was so much more.

An invitation. A demand. An imposition even.

But more than anything, it was a choice. Her younger sister was reaching out to her for the very first time, and Evie didn't know just how she felt about that.

"It came in a package of things she sent me from California," Hannah explained. "I'd forgotten a few things when I left and, well, now that I'm permanently settled back here, she sent them along."

"Along with this," Evie said. She took the envelope, hating the way her heart sped up just by the weight of it in her hands. It was a letter, not a card, and she judged there to be more than one page. "Thank you."

She stuffed it into her own bag, to deal with later. She didn't want to think about it, or all it represented. She didn't know her own mother, much less this other family her mother had. She was perfectly content with her own family, the one she'd grown up with, the one she knew. Hannah and their father and her cousins and everyone here in Oyster Bay, most of whom were here in this very room. Did her mother know she was starting a new job tomorrow, or that she'd graduated at the top of her program? Or that she'd fallen in love for the first time this summer, but that she wasn't even sure it was love, because she'd never experienced it firsthand, and what she'd heard from other people seemed irrational and sometimes downright miserable? Of course her mother didn't know any of this. Her mother had left. Made her choice. And no amount of wishing and hoping could change someone's behavior. Hannah might have gone searching for more all those years ago, but Evie was more practical than that.

Still, that didn't stop her from being…curious. Yes, she was allowed to be curious.

More than one page? What was there to tell? Her life story? Details of their mother? Descriptions of her hobbies and interests? And would Evie be expected to write back? Of course she would. Eventually, she would be expected to talk on the phone. And Evie wasn't a phone person, especially when it came to talking to a stranger.

A stranger. That's what her half-sister was. Her mother, too.

She itched the back of her neck. Not good.

"I wasn't sure when I should give it to you," Hannah said nervously.

"It's fine," Evie said, even though it wasn't, not really. Hannah and Kelly had a relationship. Hannah had another kid sister that she knew and maybe even loved. Evie wasn't part of that mix. She'd been left behind. First by their mother, then, later by Hannah. And now, Hannah was encouraging Kelly to reach out to her, it seemed. To ease her guilt? To bring her into the fold? Or was this her way of continuing to pursue the big happy family that never existed?

She'd analyze this to death later. God knew it would be all she thought about tonight now.

Hannah looked relieved as her boyfriend Dan came

over, all full of smiles and congratulation to Evie, before letting Hannah know that his daughter, Lucy, was asking for her. Evie gave her sister a nod of approval. Hannah was moving on with her life, even if she was still living under their childhood roof, same as Evie. They'd gone off in search of bigger things but both had ended up right where they'd started, in their pink and blue bedrooms.

Well, but now Hannah was back with her high school sweetheart, and Evie... She sighed. She was destined to always be the bridesmaid, wasn't she? It was just as well that she had that letter in her bag, bringing Kelly forefront to her mind. It beat thinking about Liam, and how it felt to be...

Ha. She'd almost thought in love, but no, that wasn't it. It couldn't be it. After all, Liam didn't even know her, not really. He knew Evie the bartender. Evie the bartender had casual relationships and was adult enough not to care when they ended. But the real Evie...she did care. Much as she wished she didn't.

Evie set down her champagne and looked around the room, wondering if anyone would notice if she slipped out, and decided that it was safe. Her father had invited half the town, not that the town was big, and everyone was huddled in groups, drinks in hand, the din so loud you could barely make out the music that Chip piped in over speakers. Sing along music, Evie called it, and some of the regulars certainly did, especially after one too many cocktails. Ron especially liked to croon the sappy ones, saying they made him think about Jill.

She smiled when she saw her father chatting happily with her cousin Bridget and her husband Jack, and smiled a little more when she saw Ron throw his head back for a good, loud laugh. Hannah was holding Lucy's hand, and Abby was over in the corner with her boyfriend, Zach.

She slipped out the back, took the stairs all the way down the craggy rocks until she hit the sand and slipped off her sandals. If her father asked, she'd tell him she left early to get some rest. It wasn't a lie. Even though she'd grown up in this town and knew every year-round resident, working side by side with them was something new, and her stomach was getting that familiar, funny feeling that happened every time she stepped outside her comfort zone. A new job. A new chance.

Time to pull out her list. She dropped onto the sand, setting her tote at her side, and rifled through the contents, pushing aside that envelope as quickly as her fingers grazed it, and happily retrieved the small, spiral-bound notebook where she kept her list. Everything she needed to keep herself focused and on track was on this list. The good, the bad, the things she wanted to avoid.

With a click of her pen she flicked to a fresh page. First item: Set out clothes for tomorrow. After all, there was never a second opportunity to make a bold, first impression! Two: Get a full eight hours of sleep. Ten if possible. After all, what was she doing with the rest of the night? Hannah would be off with Dan and Lucy and her cousins were all either married or attached. Sarah and a few of the girls she was friends with in town were single, but it was Sunday night, and besides, all they wanted to talk about was the lack of romantic prospects in this town. And who needed to talk about that, even if it was true?

Three: Stop thinking about Liam. It had become a habit, when she was walking on the beach, or sitting with a book as the waves lapped the shore, her personal favorite pastime. Or when Hannah casually mentioned something that Dan had said, or when she saw the way that Hannah looked at him, sort of like the way she used to look at Liam. But the difference, she reminded herself, is that Dan and Hannah were the real thing, whereas Liam was a short-term fling, something without a future, and they both knew it, from start to finish. She had to stop thinking about him. Stop wishing for something that couldn't happen. Liam was in New York and she was in Oyster Bay and that, as they said, was that.

Back to the list. Four. She tapped her pen and looked out over the ocean. There were many things she could write, things like reconsidering a private practice or even moving back to Boston and trying again there, taking the conventional route she'd always planned for herself, but being back here, with her sister and cousins and father, that no longer seemed quite so appealing. But there was only one thing that kept coming back to her over and over. Something she should do. Something that couldn't be avoided.

Four: Read Kelly's letter.

And she would. She absolutely would. But not right now.

She closed her eyes, felt the breeze in her face, and dared for a moment to go back to those carefree days of the summer, when she'd stopped trying, maybe even stopped caring, and just lived for today instead of tomorrow. When right here on this very sand, she would meet Liam after her shift, keep the conversation light, even flirty, and put all that nonsense about Boston behind her. When she was with him, those two, fleeting weeks, each day felt like an escape, from the pressure she'd put on herself, from the disappointment at how she'd ended up. Liam didn't know about all that, and she was happy not to have to discuss it.

But now, Liam was gone, back to New York and his life there, and she was moving forward again. No more hiding behind the bar at The Lantern. No more hiding on this beach, nursing white wine and getting giddy at the sight of a handsome man leaning in to kiss her. It had been fun. Fun! Yes, it had been fun. And now it was time to get back to reality.

Tomorrow would be a fresh start. Time to put those summer nights behind her.

*

Kelly rounded the bend, the final stretch to her apartment so close, she could nearly reach out and touch it, so why did she feel like she should just quit? Her legs ached nearly as much as her feet and she was panting so hard she wasn't sure she'd ever catch her breath again.

What had she been thinking, taking up jogging? She hated to sweat nearly as much as she hated the reflection of herself she caught in every store window—the form of an amateur, and someone who would be infinitely better off on the bike at the gym, or better yet, in the Pilates studio.

Only she couldn't go back to the gym, could she? At least not yet, anyway. Not until the ache in her chest had subsided, and the pain of seeing that…that louse with that…that hussy stopped making her want to smash something.

Right. With that, she kept one eye trained on the door to the walk-up she shared with five other tenants, and sprinted the rest of the way, wishing for a split second that she didn't live in San Francisco with all its steep inclines.

Still, good for the calves, at least, it should be, given the way they were now throbbing.

Panting, she pulled open the door to the vestibule, embracing the air-conditioning, and stopped outside her mailbox, remembering that she hadn't checked it the day before. She'd been too busy binge watching a BBC mini-series and indulging in not one, but two pints of ice cream, hence the run.

But now, as she stared at the flat metal box, a label with the name K. Myers across the top, her heart began to pound for reasons other than overexertion.

It had been over a week since she'd mailed the package to her sister Hannah. More than a week since she wondered if Hannah gave the letter to her other sister, Evie.

Her other sister. Just the words seemed almost surreal.

Back when Hannah lived here, she would latch onto any story Hannah told about her childhood, eager for any insight into the past she'd never been a part of. She imagined what it would have been like if she'd been there too, included in the sibling rituals of sleepover parties in each other's rooms, and tiptoeing downstairs at two in the morning on Christmas to see the presents under the tree, and collecting shells on the sand and showering in the outdoor stall behind the garage in the summer.

Instead she'd been an only child, with a mother who seemed to resent her role and a father who was too busy working half the time to notice.

Having Hannah in her life had been a dream come true. A sister. A sibling. A girl with the same brown eyes as hers! But now Hannah was gone, back in Oyster Bay, and for good, it would seem. Back with her real sister. Kelly's other sister.

She took a deep breath and blew it out before turning the key in the mailbox. She rifled through the contents quickly: a home decorating catalogue that she didn't recall signing up for, a cell phone bill, credit card statement, and a postcard advertising a romantic getaway for two in Sonoma...

She'd drop that one right into the recycling bin.

With a heavy heart, she closed and locked her mailbox. Of course Evie wouldn't have written yet. It was too soon. The post didn't move that quickly.

But certainly Evie would have received the letter by now. And Hannah emailed and texted regularly. Maybe she'd ask...see if Hannah had anything to say about the smart, blonde-haired woman who was the middle sister in their strange little family.

Or maybe she wouldn't say anything at all. Maybe she'd just wait it out. Open another pint of ice cream and binge watch a new show to keep her mind off things.

And maybe she'd go for another jog, tomorrow, before work.

She'd taken a chance. Put herself out there at long last. She'd done something she'd wanted to do for years. Connect with Evie, form a relationship, wave hello.

It was all in her sister's hands, she decided, as she climbed the stairs to her top-floor apartment, her thighs shaking a bit from her run. Of course Evie would reach out to her eventually! After all, Evie was a licensed therapist. She had a compassionate heart. Surely she wouldn't leave her waiting too long...

She'd waited twenty-five years. What difference would a few more days matter?

Chapter Two

The office of the *Oyster Bay Gazette* was located in the heart of town, just a few blocks from The Lantern and close enough to the bookstore that Evie imagined she could easily pop in on her lunch break. Evie arrived with her sister ten minutes before the start of the work day and was shocked to see that the entire front lobby was full of balloons.

Humbled, and frankly embarrassed, she looked at Sarah, the office assistant, and said in a low voice, "This really is too much. But thank you!"

Sarah's expression turned a little ruddy as she glanced from Hannah to Evie and then at the handful of balloons she was trying to tie to the edge of her waiting room located desk.

"Actually, these are for Jim. I'm not supposed to say anything, but it's so obvious something is going on that I'm not sure how I can really be expected to keep quiet. He's leaving today."

"Leaving!" Evie blinked quickly, trying to process what this meant. Jim Stafford had offered her the job, after all. He was editor in chief. How could he possibly be leaving? "Who will replace him?"

She looked fearfully at Hannah, wondering if it was too late to ask her dad for her job back but knowing that it was. The summer season was over. Business at The Lantern would slow until May, when the tourists came back, eager for lobster rolls and crab cakes and a laid-back atmosphere. The seasonal staff was gone, back in their liberal arts colleges in Vermont or Massachusetts or Rhode Island, and unless she wanted to officially become a charity case, it was time for Evie to step aside.

Besides, she didn't want to continue tending bar. She couldn't! She had a graduate degree. From a good college! All those years spent studying, maintaining a perfect grade point average, only to lose out on that opportunity in Boston and now, possibly lose out on this column on her first day?

Maybe she'd ask Bridget for a job at the Harper House Inn. Ever since Bridget had turned her childhood home into a bed and breakfast, business had grown. Abby had been added to the staff and was now running the kitchen. Maybe Bridget could squeeze her in too?

Doing what?

She itched her forehead. Took a deep breath. She needed to calm down and fast unless she wanted the hives to start spreading down her cheeks and neck. And from recent experience, she knew they would.

"A new guy is starting today," Sarah said casually as she secured the balloons and stepped back to smile at them in satisfaction. "I haven't met him yet, but I've heard he's experienced. And Jim promised that all positions would be safe."

Oh, thank God. Evie realized her hand was shaking as she went to scratch a hive. Really, she was behaving like one of her patients, not the calm, cool professional that she was! And what would she tell her patients in this situation? One day at a time, don't get too ahead of yourself.

In other words, calm your ass down.

"Well of course all positions will be safe!" Hannah laughed. "This is Oyster Bay, not Manhattan. It's not like there's exactly a line out the door of qualified journalists or photographers."

True. All true. Leave it to Hannah to be the voice of reason here. Really, if Evie had been thinking clearly, she would have said the same to herself. If there was one good thing about being back in Oyster Bay instead of Boston, where she'd spent both undergrad and grad school and had hoped to spend many more years, it was that here she had job security.

She had a lot of security, actually. It was a safe place. A little boring, sure. Safe, but certainly lacking in surprises.

She sighed. No use feeling sorry for herself again. Today was supposed to be a fresh start. And surprises were highly overrated. A nice, stable existence had always been her preference. Routine was her friend. Her boring friend, but a trustworthy one.

"There's going to be a party at the end of the day," Sarah continued. "I'm in charge of ordering from Angie's. And at that time the new boss will be introduced."

"Could be worse," Hannah said. "And Jim's wife has been trying to get him to retire and move south since before I moved away."

True, very true. Luellen had been talking about a future in the Carolinas since Evie was still studying for the SATs.

Hannah nudged her elbow. "Come on. I'll show you to your desk."

Evie followed her sister down the long hallway, past one messy desk after another, some piled so high with papers that Evie felt herself twitch, and she wondered if she might eventually hold a seminar on the power of organization in the workplace. One desk had five bumper stickers slapped to it, with contradictory yet equally polarizing political statements, and Evie ran through the residents of Oyster Bay, as well as everyone she knew on staff here, trying to place its owner.

She settled on Tony Calisi. Yes, it would be Tony. Back in school he had once staged a protest against the principal's insistence to include only healthy snacks in the vending machines, and he'd initiated a march when the dress code was enforced, claiming that girls should be allowed to wear their shorts as short as they wanted, and really, clothing should be completely optional, considering it was a free country and all that.

And now, he was her colleague.

Don't read too much into that, she told herself. After all, Tony was well rounded. He'd played drums and the guitar and he'd rallied the troupes! He had causes. And...maybe he'd changed.

Her gaze lingered on one of the anarchy stickers. Or...maybe not.

"Here you are," Hannah said, stopping near the back window, to a perfectly clean desk that faced the boss's office if the brass plate bearing Jim's name gave anything away. Noticing Evie's stare, Hannah shrugged and said, "You're the new hire. No one wants to sit across from the big boss. Coffee's in the kitchen next to the conference room. I have to run out and take some photos of the new dock project before the rain hits. You going to be okay?"

Evie smiled. It was just like her first day of school, when Hannah walked her all the way to her kindergarten classroom and then ditched her to hang with the second graders. Evie had stood and watched while all the other children clung to their mothers' hands, and the mothers hovered with anxious expressions, their foreheads creased, their eyes brimming with actual tears. Even at the age of five, Evie had known she was different, and even though she felt sad that day, and a little lonely, she knew she had a father and a sister and an aunt and an uncle and three great cousins who let her call their paternal grandmother Mimi, just like they did. She didn't need a mother. She would be fine, just fine.

And she had been. Sort of.

"I think I'll survive," she said, sliding into her chair. After all, it was just a job. If Tony Calisi could handle it, then surely she could! Outside the window, she heard a rumble of thunder. "You'd better hurry."

"I'll be back in time for the party. It's pretty much the most excitement we've had around here since…well…never. It's Oyster Bay, after all." Hannah shook her head and sailed down the hall, disappearing over the cubicle walls and houseplants.

Evie smiled at all her new colleagues, all of whom she'd known since she was a child. There was Tony arriving now, who, judging by the ripped jeans and blue-tinged hair, had certainly not evolved since he was eighteen. And Matthew Gordon, who lived six doors down and used to swing on their tree swing and not let them have a turn until he was finished, even though it was their swing and their tree.

Really, what was there to be so nervous about? This place was full of familiar faces. Like Hannah had said, it was Oyster Bay, where nothing was unexpected.

*

At four o'clock Evie looked up from the response she had drafted to her first, and so far only, letter—sent at eleven last night from Ron, thinly disguised as Don. With her first article scheduled to go into Wednesday's edition, she could only hope that a few more letters came in tonight or tomorrow morning, or she'd be advising her readers on why it wasn't a good idea to, yet again, park outside your soon-to-be ex-wife's new boyfriend's house with a bouquet of flowers.

Shaking her head, she sent the response off to "Don" all the same, hoping that at least he would benefit from it, and wandered into the conference room, where, sure enough, a spread from Angie's Café was set out on the table, along with a beautiful cake that for whatever reason said, "Happy Birthday, Jim!"

"They messed up," Sarah said hurriedly, her cheeks flushing a dark pink as she took a plastic knife and scraped away the letters. "I didn't realize until I opened the box just a few minutes ago."

"I'm sure that Jim will understand," Evie said.

"Maybe, but I'm not so sure about the new boss. Tony already met him, you know. He bumped into him having lunch with Jim at Dunley's. Said he's a real shark. Some guy from New York. He apparently wants to turn the paper into something bigger. Widen the distribution. Bring it online. Maybe even take it…regional."

Sarah's expression revealed just how crazy she thought that was, and Evie mildly agreed, despite how exciting the thought of a bigger audience was. Maybe this wouldn't just be a "fun" job after all. Maybe she'd really reach people.

"Any other details about him?" She couldn't help but feel anxious. Her column was new, and if this guy had plans in mind for the paper, she couldn't be sure that her article would make the cut.

"No, but you know Tony. He doesn't pay much attention to details like that. The most I got out of him was that his name is Will and he has a firm handshake." Sarah sighed and looked down at the cake, which now simply bore the name "Jim" in blue icing. "Well, I'll start cutting it as soon as everyone gathers."

"And here they come," Evie said, turning to see Hannah walk through the door, her hair still damp from the rain that fell steadily outside the window.

"I saw Ron," was the first thing she said. "He said a friend of his wrote you a letter and he seemed very eager to know if you had received it."

"Was his friend named Don by any chance?" Evie said, raising an eyebrow.

Hannah laughed. "Let me guess? Ron himself?" She smoothed her wet hair down and stared at the spread. "At least I made it back in time for the punch!"

"And cake," Sarah said, pulling a face as she gestured to the rather sad-looking confection whose frosting was smeared where the rest of the lettering had been. A glob of icing sat on a paper plate, most unappetizing. Suddenly, she stood straighter, her blue eyes widening. "They're coming, they're coming." She positioned herself in front of the cake in a vain attempt to hide it. "Act natural!"

Evie smiled and turned toward the door as the room fell quiet, but the grin slipped from her face when she saw the two men approach and she knew that there was nothing natural about this moment. Her heart started beating and her mind was working overtime, trying to process what it was seeing, and she instinctively inched backwards, until her hand landed in something warm and soft. The frosting that Sarah had scraped off the cake.

She looked up at her new boss, wondering if he'd noticed, or if she was just a face in the (albeit) small crowd, but luck was not on her side today. It hadn't been for a while. There was a glimmer in his eye. A spark. A recognition.

It was Liam. Liam being short for William. Liam who had told her he was returning to his job at the publishing house in New York. Liam who had kissed her good-bye and then lingered on the beach, long enough to make her wonder if she should turn around, say something, or go back, kiss him, all the while knowing that there was no point, that his life was there and that her life was here and that therefore there could be no future.

Only now Liam was here. In Oyster Bay. In the conference room of the town newspaper. And he'd never even told her that he was coming back. Much less staying for good.

So much for that nice, stable life she'd counted on. It looked like Oyster Bay did have its share of surprises after all.

Chapter Three

Evie didn't know how she got through the next fifteen minutes. She stood, alongside her sister, her mouth curved in a cool, pleasant, entirely professional hint of a smile while she listened to Jim explain his reasons for leaving, and "William's" reason for coming on board. She listened as Liam described, in his smooth, deep voice, his work history, his position in New York, the fact that starting tomorrow the *Gazette* would be online, targeting a wider audience. She kept her eyes trained on Jim, and his kind blue eyes behind his wire-framed glasses, dodging the pull to so much as glance in Liam's direction, even if she couldn't help but notice he was wearing a blue shirt and a plaid tie and he'd had a haircut since the last time she'd seen him, but just a bit. She focused on her breathing, keeping it measured, hoping that the itch she had behind her ear wasn't an indication that she was about to break out in hives.

Beside her she knew that Hannah's eyes were as round as her own. And she didn't need to look in Sarah's direction to know how she was reacting.

She didn't dare look at all. She kept her eyes trained on Jim, but damn it if her hands weren't shaking.

"Well, with that said, I'm sure that William would love to make the rounds and meet the team!"

Oh, no. No. Evie met her sister's eyes, and they seemed to pass an unspoken message to her. Get out. Now. Figure the rest out later.

She inched toward the door, but as she did Liam looked over, caught her eye, and she knew that there was no running, not now, at least.

He made his introductions brief, moving along the line from person to person, but time seemed to slow down as he approached her, his gaze cool and steady, his expression unreadable.

"William Bauer," he said, extending a hand to her.

She wiped the remains of the frosting onto her napkin, but it did little good. She extended her left hand instead, and held it, awkwardly, as if she was someone regal. Normally, they might have laughed at this, but today there was wariness in Liam's eyes, and a distance that made her unsettled.

So this was how it was going to be then? They would just pretend that all those summer nights had never happened? That he'd never kissed her mouth, her neck, and that little spot behind her ear that she never knew existed until she met him?

"Evie Donovan," she said. She took his hand, her body seeming to react all on its own to the warmth of his palm, and she idly wondered if he'd hold onto her for a moment, maybe even…caress it.

But nope. He gave it a good hard shake that surprised her so much, she jerked her hand away.

"And your role here?" My, he was cutting right to it, wasn't he?

Her heart was pounding. "I'll be writing the new advice column."

Liam's brow twitched, just an inch, but enough for her to notice. But then, that's what she did. She noticed things. Like how the flecks around Liam's pupils were gold and how he was clean shaven, not sporting the more casual, scruffy look he'd had when she'd last seen him, when she could feel the rough texture against her chin when she leaned in to…

Oh, no. Uh-uh. This was no longer Liam from those summer nights. This was William. Her boss.

"Advice column?" Was that a hint of mischief that shone in his eyes? A bit of a smile that curved his mouth?

"It's my first day," she said, for lack of anything else to say.

"Well then, we have something in common, don't we?"

If there was any doubt that he was insinuating

something with that comment, the lift of his eyebrow put it to rest.

Evie waited until he had turned to the next person in the room, and excused herself to the restroom, muttering something about needing to wash her hands, where she hid in a toilet stall for the next thirty minutes, a tactic she'd mastered back in high school, when she'd agreed to go to school dances just to keep her father from worrying about her not being invited. Back then, she kept a book on hand for moments like this, but today, even her phone was back at her desk.

She didn't emerge until the door swung open and, though she had planned on hiding there until she'd figured out a plan (Perhaps a sudden bout of stomach flu that required her to be out of commission until she'd applied for and secured another job, or calling her father and asking for her bartending gig back? Ron would be thrilled. Or maybe she'd just pack her bags and return to Boston, shack up on a friend's couch until she'd been accepted somewhere.), she was forced out of the handicap stall when Sarah called out, "Evie? You in here?"

Really, where else would she be? And so, with a heave of dread, she walked over to the toilet and flushed it for show and then marched to the sinks to wash her hands, even though they'd been perfectly clean since she scrubbed the frosting from them.

She caught Sarah's reflection in the mirror, briefly, but

long enough to know that this conversation was about to
go exactly as she'd feared.

"Isn't that the guy from Bridget and Jack's wedding?"
Sarah was blinking so hard that Evie was struggling to
maintain eye contact.

Or maybe she was struggling because she didn't want
to admit that yes, it was, of course it was. The man she
had met first at her cousin Bridget's rehearsal dinner and
then the man who had rearranged seating to ensure a
chair beside hers at the wedding reception, surprising
everyone at the table, but most of all, her. A man who
had then invited her to the beach, not just one night, but
many nights. A man who had made her understand what
people meant when they said they were in love. A man
who had made her want things she hadn't considered
wanting before. A man who was not the safe choice or
the sure bet or, like her last boyfriend, a lab partner
whose common interest was centered in their studies and
their love of Woody Allen films.

Evie stared at her reflection in the mirror, wondering
just what Liam thought of her now. She was hardly the
girl he'd met in August, wearing a cocktail dress and
shoes that gave her blisters. Today her blonde hair was
pulled back in a low ponytail and she wore her thick-
framed glasses—librarian glasses, Hannah called them—
and a pale pink button-down shirt that was entirely
professional. And slacks. God help her, she was wearing
slacks.

Well, she thought, stiffening and walking over to the

wall to crank out a long sheet of paper towels. What did it matter? That was then and this was…a disaster.

"Yep, that's him."

"Did you know he was taking this job?" Sarah's eyes were round.

"No," Evie said, and for some reason, that hurt. It confirmed everything she knew in her heart, that the time they'd spent together hadn't meant anything beyond what it was, a fleeting two weeks, and reminded her that maybe she had dared to care a little more than she should have.

After all, if he'd wanted to continue where they left off, wouldn't he have called? Yes, he would have. And it didn't take a psych degree to figure that out.

"Oh." Sarah looked a little coy as she leaned in to apply lipstick. "I guess we all thought…"

Evie frowned. Hannah knew. Of course Hannah knew. Evie had confided in her before Liam left. But the others? This wasn't good. "Thought what?"

"That you two seemed so cozy at the wedding reception. We all just thought maybe something happened between the two of you."

Something had happened. But that was past tense. And right now, Liam was her boss. And Sarah's.

Her stomach dropped so low she had to set a hand on it. "He was only in town for a visit." Evasion, a tactic usually used by patients, but one that came in handy in times like this.

Sarah shrugged and dropped her lipstick tube back

into her handbag. "If you say so."

"I do." Evie pulled in a breath, trying to steady herself, even though her mind was spinning. What happened between her and Liam was irrelevant now. It may have been a big deal to her, a rare, and okay, downright magical two weeks, but Liam was a successful and handsome New Yorker, who had probably been on many dinner dates since she'd last seen him.

"Then you won't mind if I—"

"What?" Oops. Evie's tone was a little snappier than she'd intended.

Sarah didn't seem to pick up on it as she fluffed her hair and checked her profile from both sides. She smoothed her floral printed and much more age appropriate and figure flattering skirt over her hips as her blue eyes lit up. "I don't know…if I flirt with him a bit?"

Evie counted to three and trained her expression on her reflection, careful to keep her face clinical, to not emote a thing, even if inside she was practically screaming. Was Sarah even kidding? Only a month ago she and Liam were side by side at Gull Point, their toes in the sand, the wind in their hair, and no one else around for miles, and now Sarah, her friend Sarah, wanted to *flirt* with him?

But what could she say? That she was still hung up on him? "Isn't that against company policy?"

"I don't know," Sarah said with a wrinkle of her brow. She considered it for a moment before a mischievous grin curved the corners of her mouth. "But he's the boss. I suppose it's up to him to decide!"

Good grief. Evie felt the dread roll through her, and she didn't even realize that Sarah was now standing in an open doorway, looking at her expectantly. "You coming?"

Evie internally whimpered but nodded her head all the same. After all, what choice did she have?

*

Liam dropped into the chair behind his new desk and adjusted the seat position. The office had cleared out, the staff had happily accepted the offer to leave early after the cake was boxed up, and only Sarah, the receptionist and a face he remembered from the two weeks he'd spent in this town over the summer, had lingered a few extra minutes. She was being helpful, maybe just trying to kiss up to the new boss, but there was something else, something more, something that made him excuse himself to his office, the door firmly closed behind him.

He knew the look. He'd seen it many times over the years, back at the publishing house and other places too, like the gym, or holiday parties, or the few dates his friends had urged him to go on. He'd go, once pressed enough, and sometimes he even had a little fun, sometimes he'd even suggest a second date, or a third, but when he saw that look he'd know that it had been a mistake. He couldn't offer these women what they were looking for. The most he could offer was some fun. Some flirtation. Something that never went much below the surface level. Something safe.

Anything more made his stomach knot. Made the guilt come back, and the sadness, and the fear. Stone cold fear.

His wife was dead. And what kind of man would it make him to just replace her? He'd made promises. Vows. He'd honored them. But in the end, it hadn't been enough.

Pushing away the dark thoughts before they took over, he rifled through the personnel files until he came to the one he was looking for. Donovan, Evie. Her byline photo reflected the same woman he had seen this afternoon: hair off the face, black-framed glasses shielding those blue eyes, and a friendly but ever so slight curve to those full lips.

He pulled in a breath. The woman he had known let her hair blow in the breeze. She didn't pry into his past and she didn't talk about the future, two things that kept their time together pleasant. Too pleasant. So pleasant that he'd struggled not to think about her when he went back to New York, and made him almost dread the thought of seeing her again nearly as much as he looked forward to it. She was easy to talk to, and at the time, he'd attributed that to her being a bartender. Now he realized it was because she was a therapist.

And now, she was his employee. So much for avoiding her when he came back to town, as he had hoped to do.

He skimmed her resume, which was brief but impressive. Instead of listing The Lantern, she listed clinical hours, a master's degree program, community service hours at a women's shelter, a transcript with a near flawless grade point average.

In other words, qualities he looked for in a long-term relationship.

Would have looked for. If…

So many ifs.

He closed the folder and set it back in the file cabinet and then looked around his new office. At the place that that was supposed to be his escape. His fresh start. The place where he didn't think about his past and made a stab at some semblance of a future.

But all he could think about was Evie, and how she'd attracted him with her quiet and easy manner and made the time he'd spent here a little less lonely than he'd expected it to be.

She was shy, and sincere, and she didn't push for anything. She was aloof, even a little distant, keeping him in that safe zone as, against his will, he'd wished for more. He'd told himself when he came back he'd cut it off, call it for what it was, a fling, a casual thing that could never be anymore. He told himself they came from different worlds, that it couldn't work anyway, that she was a bartender, that maybe she made a habit of keeping things casual.

But he was wrong. So wrong. About all of it.

He glanced at her folder one more time before standing up and flicking off his overhead light.

Well. It looked like he hadn't been the only one
keeping secrets this summer after all.

Chapter Four

Evie had two letters in her inbox when she arrived at work the next morning, her glasses swapped out for contacts, her lips covered in gloss that she'd snagged from Hannah's cosmetics bag. Her pride checked at the door of her childhood bedroom.

The black skirt she wore was hugging her hips in the most uncomfortable way, but she reasoned that it was simply professional attire, as were the black power pumps that she'd snagged from Hannah's closet, with her consent, of course. Hannah had all but thrust a sleeveless blouse in her direction too, her smile so suggestive that Evie almost gave back the shoes. Almost. Instead, she'd muttered something about not having had time to go shopping for the new job yet, and left the room to cross the hall to her own, where she closed the door and breathed heavily, knowing that her sister wouldn't buy her lies much longer.

Her heart was beating quickly as she glanced in the direction of Liam's office. The door was closed, and she was happy for that, even if the little tug in her chest said otherwise for a moment. Rationally, this was for the best. With any luck, it would remain that way until she figured out what to do about all this. Or at least until close of business.

Right. Time to read the letters.

Ah, the first one was from Beverly Wright, her very own next-door neighbor, who had a fondness of spying on the family through the hole she kept groomed in the hedge dividing their two backyards. Bev's son, Timmy, was the light of her life, and much as she loved him, she was a tad overeager about finding another woman to share him with, if one would have him.

Dear Evie,

I am most concerned about my son, who I feel should be married and maybe even expecting his first child by now. There is nothing wrong with him—quite the opposite! He is tall, handsome, kind, and very successful. He works for a family business here in town that he will inherit someday—tell me what woman with any sense would turn down such a catch? I've tried to set him up on dates, but from what I have witnessed, no woman in this town has come close to deserving the many qualities that my son can offer!

Here Evie stopped to roll her eyes. Over the summer Bev had tried to set Hannah up with Timmy and had been dismayed when Hannah reunited with her high school sweetheart instead.

She continued reading. Tim a catch. Tim was amazing. And she, Bev, would make the "perfect mother-in-law!" Here Evie actually laughed out loud, catching the attention of Tony Calisi, who looked at her suspiciously.

While many women can be overbearing when it comes to their sons, I am quite the opposite, knowing when to step back and never pushing! After all, it's only natural for me to want grandchildren…

It was signed, "Searching for Mrs. Right."

Mrs. Right or Mrs. Wright? Evie sighed. Tim wasn't so bad, even if he had been a bit of a creep back in grade school, hiding under the bleachers to look up girls' skirts and occasionally even sneaking into the girls locker room before gym class let out.

Still, there weren't many girls in town who weren't aware of Tim's reputation. There was Sarah, the newest member of the community who had a thing for alpha males who would break her heart and, of course, there were those who hadn't been in the same grade as Tim, and might not have heard the stories Evie had—

Evie felt the blood drain from her face. Wait. No. She skimmed the letter again, reading it this time with the eyes of a true cynic. Bev couldn't be thinking that *she* would be interested in Tim? No, no, no.

Evie pressed the backspace bar on her keyboard until the perfectly encouraging response she had been composing was now nothing more than a flashing blinker. Rather than condone Bev's meddling in her son's love life, or lack thereof, she would instead put a stop to it once and for all. The women of Oyster Bay would thank her. Timmy, no doubt, would too.

Dear Searching,

It is every parent's wish to see their children happy; however, from personal experience, I know that oftentimes what makes the child is happy is not what the parent thinks should make them happy. Take a step back, support your son's decisions, even if that means he doesn't currently wish to date at the moment. Have you considered taking up knitting? It will do wonders to lessen your anxiety over your son's romantic fate. Getting involved in the community is a wonderful outlet for focusing on your life, which will give your son the courage he needs to pursue his own life.

Evie fluttered her lashes and clicked on the next letter. Another from "Don" describing a run-in with his wife and her new boyfriend at Dunley's last night.

Evie pursed her lips and powered off a response. *A run-in or a stakeout, Don? Instead of stalking your wife, try using that time in a more positive way. If you don't trust yourself to fight the temptation, then keep busy, and commit your free time to something less destructive. Sign up for an evening class, or take a dance lesson, or meet a friend for dinner. I promise you that once you are busy focusing on your own life, you will stop focusing on Jill's.*

Oops. She pressed the backspace button until Jill's name disappeared from the screen, and then, with a click of a button, sent off her response. That left three options for tomorrow's edition. She decided to go with Bev's email. It tapped into the most universal topic, and one that she could relate to, on a less intense scale. After all, wasn't the surprise party the other night proof that her dad's intentions weren't always aligned with her wishes? Still, his heart was always in the right place.

With that taken care of, she glanced in the direction of Liam's office, her heart gaining speed when she saw that it was now open, just enough that she could make out the back of his head, and that hair...that thick, dark, silky hair that she had run her fingers through. She'd never known she could find a man's hair so appealing! Back in Boston, dating had been more about companionship, not the excited, nervous, funny feeling she got every time she heard Liam's voice or thought of his face, or anticipated another picnic in the sand...

What you like about him is his appearance, Evie, she reminded herself. It was a chemical reaction. That was all. What more could it be? After all, she had only known him for two weeks!

Make that two glorious, amazing, impossible to forget two weeks, she thought, smiling dreamily into the distance.

Her eyes snapped open as she hitched herself straighter in her chair. He was there. In the doorway of his office, and crap, crap, crap, he was staring at her. She jerked her head to the left, then realized she was staring at a cubicle wall, so she jerked it to the right, and again, the same thing. She stared at her computer screen, waiting a proper three seconds before slowly looking up, and only then releasing a long sigh of relief when he was no longer there.

She felt a tap on her shoulder and jumped. Laughing at herself, she swiveled in her chair, expecting to find Hannah, and then, well, there was nothing funny about this. It was Liam. Looking down at her.

"Yes?" she croaked.

"Got a minute?" He tipped his head in the direction of his office door and, because she didn't have a window-facing cubicle and therefore couldn't plan a quick escape and never return, she did as her boss asked and followed him, heart pounding, to his office.

Christ. He closed the door.

She stared at the knob for a few seconds, the dread twisting her stomach into such knots that she had to sit down, even though he hadn't asked her to. Yet.

He walked around her and sat down at his own desk. She did a quick scan of it. No picture frames or personal memorabilia, though it was only his second day of work. And hers. Still, maybe he was all business. Maybe that was why he had called her in here. Maybe he didn't want to discuss anything other than her column.

She met his eyes, and she knew by the way they lingered, with a thrill that bordered on fear, that this wasn't the case at all.

"So." He gave her a lopsided grin, the slow kind that made her stomach flip-flop and her senses disappear.

"About this summer—"

"That was extremely uncharacteristic of me," Evie hurried to say. And it had been. All of it. From losing out on the job in Boston to going from hostess to bartender and actually enjoying it. To the evenings spent with Liam, a stranger from New York, whom she assumed she would never see again and yet didn't let that stand in her way. For the first time in her life, she had lived in the present, not thinking of the future, not worrying about it or planning for it.

And now it was payback time.

"Same," Liam said firmly, and Evie frowned.

"What do you mean by that?" she asked.

He gave her a funny look, pausing for a moment. "Nothing. I just mean, it wasn't like me to...do that." He reached for a mug of coffee and took a long sip. A nice way to buy time, she thought.

Suddenly she forgot that she was sitting in her boss's office, a place that up until a matter of seconds ago, she was afraid to enter. Now, facing the man who had kissed her, laughed with her, and touched her, she felt on equal footing. And she wasn't pleased.

"So I was just a good-time girl, then?"

He sputtered on the coffee and set the mug down firmly. "That's not what I said."

"No, but what we had was...casual." That was one word for it. "And you just said that was out of character."

"It was."

"So you usually only get involved with girls you take seriously?" Girls who weren't bartenders or interested in fleeting, summer flings? In other words, girls like her?

"I didn't mean that," he said tersely. He shifted in his seat. A-ha! He was uncomfortable. Well, rightfully so.

"And what did you mean?" She tipped her head and waited, folded her hands in her lap, and gave the serene smile she gave to all the patients during her clinical hours. And Bev Wright when she was talking up poor Tim.

He cleared his throat and reached for a folder, and suddenly all talk of their relationship, or lack thereof, vanished. It was her file. The one with her resume. Her complete educational and work history, minus her bartending stint. The cover letter where she described herself as goal-oriented, self-motivated, and driven. "So." He cocked an eyebrow."It seems that there was more to you than you led on."

"As I said, we were keeping it casual." Oh, but there was nothing casual about it, at least not to her. Being with Liam, it was the first time in her life that she actually got it, that she understood what made men like Ron stalk their cheating wives, or people like Hannah find it in her heart to reunite with Dan Fletcher, after more than a decade since last speaking. Liam wasn't just a fling. He was…an awakening.

She jutted her chin, determined to stay strong. She'd done nothing wrong. She hadn't lied. It wasn't in her nature to lie. Omit, sure, and okay, maybe that did fall somewhere under the scope of being less than truthful, or at least forthcoming, but all that would have come out in good time.

Or so she told herself.

The truth was that it had been fun to let Liam see her for the girl he thought she was. Fun-loving, carefree, causal Evie, who poured Long Island iced teas at The Lantern and mixed a mean martini (even if she did have to practice a dozen times in the kitchen with the help of a phone app to get it just right, and even if, admittedly, she'd never tasted one herself). And really, was it such a lie? So she had a degree. She'd bombed in Boston. Failed to secure a position in her field the way her classmates had. Ended up in her hometown working for her dad.

Really, she had been very honest with him. The rest was just…back story.

"Besides," she said, lifting her chin a little higher. "I can say the same for you. After all, here you are. And this is quite a surprise." She chuckled, even though it was far from funny.

She could tell by the way he was struggling to make eye contact that he was being evasive, or maybe feeling a little ashamed.

Or maybe she was giving the man far too much credit. Seeing the person she wished he was. Thought he was. He was merely uncomfortable. So was she, not that she'd be showing it.

She gave a little smile and matched his brow lift, best she could.

He reached for his mug again, but then seemed to think the better of it. "I thought it would be better to explain it in a conversation."

Her heart sank. So there it was. Of course it was. The rejection. She didn't need to hear anymore, and she wanted to tell him so, but now he actually was looking at her properly, his eyes apologetic.

"I should have told you that I was coming back to town, but…Well, we hadn't made any promises."

"No," she managed to say. "We didn't."

"As for the paper, I obviously didn't know you'd taken a job here."

She nodded. "Fair enough."

"What we…what happened…" He loosened the tie around his neck. "This summer was nice. Really nice. But, I'm not looking for anything more."

With her? Or generally speaking? Her eyes narrowed on him, but her face, she worried, had started to flame. And itch. The hives! They were growing. Behind her ears and on the back of her neck and nothing she could do could make them stop.

"I never said that I was," she replied, her tone measured, even though she realized she was struggling to breathe. Her face was growing hot with humiliation, and anger, she realized. Yes, she was angry. Honestly, who did this guy think he was?

Her boss, unfortunately.

Well, not for long. She had degrees. Multiple degrees. Meaning, she had options. She just had to pursue them again. And she would. Oh, yes, she would.

"I should get back to my desk. Letters to answer and all that," she said, rising from her chair. She managed one tight smile as she reached for the doorknob. "So, we're good?"

He frowned, visibly, the space between his eyebrows folding as he looked at her. Finally, after he blinked a few times, he nodded. "Yeah. We're good."

"Great!" she said, baring her teeth into a smile and pulling the door open.

She marched all the way to the bathroom, where she intended to wash her face with cold water to fight off the growing rash, and then…then she would be hiding in the last stall until she'd figured out a new plan.

Or at least until the hives went away.

*

Kelly scooted her chair into work and cursed when she saw the time on the bottom right corner of her monitor. Seventeen minutes late because she'd had that extra glass of wine last night to try to push the thought of Brian and Shannon and how they might have spent the weekend together (dinner at the Italian place near the bridge, then drinks at the no-name place next door with French advertisement posters and the red wallpaper, the one she had first introduced Brian to, then a leisurely Sunday brunch of egg white omelets after hours of fornication on the sheet set she had bought for Brian, because he only had one set, with holes at the corner of the fitted sheet, when she met him) from her mind and then couldn't get going this morning. Seventeen minutes that had no doubt been noted by her boss.

She glanced in the direction of his door, her heart sinking when she saw that it was open, but lifting again when she saw that he was on the phone. Good. He probably hadn't even noticed. And really, it had only happened a few times...

More like a few dozen times, if she was being honest with herself.

But really, it wasn't always her fault. There was the time where the power went out in her building and her phone never charged and the battery drained and the alarm couldn't go off. What could she have done about that? Of course, this may have been overlooked if it hadn't been for the unfortunate circumstance just two days prior, when she and Brian had gotten in a big fight on the way home from the gym, when she had observed him chatting with Shannon outside the men's locker room, his body language far too suggestive, judging from the way he kept leaning in to hear her better, a wide grin on his face.

Shannon was a low talker. Kelly knew this because she actually used to be friends with Shannon. Well, maybe not friends, but friendly. They'd taken Pilates together. They'd bonded in the steam shower after a Tuesday night class. And it has been Kelly who had invited Shannon to come along with her and Brian for drinks at the no-name place that Friday night, not even giving pause to Shannon's long blonde hair and perky upturned nose and big, bright blue eyes.

Everything had seemed fine for drinks. Brian and Shannon hit it off like old friends (of course they did!) and afterward, at the next Pilates class, Shannon told Kelly that she was really lucky to have a guy like Brian and Kelly's heart had soared because yes, she was lucky, wasn't she?

The guys she'd dated in high school and college had been boys. Brian Nicholson was a man. Three years older than her, with a degree from Berkeley and a great job at a start-up software company, Brian was going places. And of course, it didn't hurt that he had soulful green eyes and a wicked grin and that he knew how to play the guitar and he played it well.

She should have known something was up when Brian started suggesting to her that they invite Shannon with them for drinks or dinner. Looking back, she realized that he was turning their dates into a group event, a really big, flashing warning, and one she had overlooked because, naïve as she was, she just thought that Brian was so friendly and inclusive, and it made her love him even more!

And after about a month of that, those group outings did become dates again. Dates for Brian and Shannon, with Kelly cut out of the mix. Out of a friend. Out of a boyfriend.

She narrowed her eyes at the computer screen as her email powered up.

"Kelly?"

She jumped at the sound of her name and looked up to see Darren standing in the doorway of his office. She swallowed hard, but her heart was pounding something fierce and she knew what this meant. No good ever came from being called into your boss's office.

He was looking at her expectantly, a bemused expression on his face. "A word?"

A word. In other words, more than one word. More like a string of words that weren't even words at all, but rather, questions and accusations.

She stood on shaking knees, ignoring the knowing glances from her fellow coworkers as she walked the twenty feet to Darren's corner office, with floor to ceiling windows that gave a view of the skyline.

He closed the door behind her. A very bad sign indeed.

"I know I was late—" she started, but Darren just held up a hand.

It was only then that she realized she wasn't alone in the room. Betsy, the head of Human Resources, was already sitting in one of the two visitor chairs positioned opposite Darren's paper-strewn desk. Her frown nearly matched Darren's, only hers was accentuated by the jowls that framed her jaw, turning her displeasure into more of a scowl.

"I can explain," Kelly began, but she could tell by the blank expressions she was met with that they didn't care to hear her excuses.

"This isn't the first time you have been late to work,"

Darren said. "And your performance has been sliding for a while."

Her performance? "I meet every deadline."

"There isn't any passion in your work," Darren replied, and at this, Kelly almost burst out laughing. Passion? She worked in the research department of a commercial real estate firm! How could she possibly be passionate about the vacancy rate in office buildings?

"We're offering you a severance," Betsy added. "It will be included in your last paycheck."

Her last paycheck. Sure, she hadn't ever loved the job, and yes, she was far from passionate about it, but the thought of leaving and never coming back was upsetting. This was her routine. This was her home away from home, as strange as that was. She opened her mouth, wanting to fight for what was hers, but again the blank expressions silenced her. There would be no arguing her case. Their decision was final.

She stood and walked out of the room, feeling like a child who had just gotten in trouble by both her parents. They'd tag teamed her! Doubled down, ganged up! Maybe if she had talked to Darren alone she could have pleaded with him, begged for another chance. But then, maybe not. He had called in Betsy, after all.

She gathered up her few belongings: her "Love What You Do!" mug that made her stop and wonder for a moment if she did do what she loved and if this was half the problem; her framed photo of her and Hannah, taken about three years ago, when she'd graduated from college and Hannah had treated her to a spa day in Napa; the box of granola bars she kept in a drawer for the days that she was (surprise, surprise!) running too late for work to grab any breakfast; and the navy, merino wool cardigan she kept draped around the back of her chair, to fight off the endless chill of the central air-conditioning.

Lindsay was giving her a wide-eyed look over the wall that divided their cubicle, and Kelly knew if she said anything, even one word, she would burst into tears. Just thinking of talking right now made her chin wobble, but she managed to push out, "I'll text you," as she crammed everything into her tote bag, grateful that it was so ridiculously large in scale, and swung it over her shoulder.

She was at the elevator bank in record time, jamming her finger against the button until a set of mirrored doors finally spread open, and then, that was it. The elevator deposited her in the lobby, and she walked outside, into the sunshine, amongst the throngs of other people who were happily going about their day, having no idea that her world was starting to crumble around her. No more lunches on a park bench with Lindsay, no more office drama like the crush that Lindsay had on Paul in marketing. No more happy hour drinks or work clothes or Starbucks runs before a big staff meeting.

She fumbled in her tote for the sunglasses. The thing was massive, it contained everything, including now all her measly office belongings.

But not sunglasses. Not today. She'd left them on her

kitchen counter, if you could count the twelve-by-twelve block of surface area as a counter at all. And now she couldn't even hide behind them. She could duck into the nearest store and buy a new pair, but that would be wasteful, considering she was now unemployed.

Unemployed. She was twenty-five, and she had just been fired.

Would anyone even hire her again after this? She started shaking, contemplating the possibility. It was like a criminal record. It was forever there. A part of her. Like a poor high school transcript that limited your college options. Her future suddenly felt even more bleak than it had this morning, if such a thing were possible.

In a fit of desperation, she decided to call her mother.

"Kelly?" her mother sounded distant and distracted. In the background a man was barking out orders to focus on your position, breathe into the stretch. In other words: bad timing.

"Hi, Loraine," she said. She'd been calling her mother by her first name since she was four, when her mother felt the need to "claim her identity once and for all" and "establish herself as her own person." Whatever that meant.

Immediately she regretted calling. She should have resisted the urge, fought the inner voice that always came out in her neediest moments, the one that said, "Go on, call your mother. She'll know what to say. That's her job. She's your mother."

Normally she resisted. Occasionally, after a third glass of wine, when her judgment was impaired, she caved. Dared to think that this time it would be different. Now, like all the other times, she was left feeling worse than before she'd called.

"Is this a bad time?" she asked, even though she knew that it was, or rather, that it was never a good time. Even as a little girl, she could remember reaching around her mother's waist for a hug at the same time her mother was grabbing her wrists and unraveling them. She was never much of a hugger, her mother. Now, when they saw each other, which was once a month for dinner, she couldn't help noticing how cold the embraces remained. No tight squeezes after a rough day. And certainly no lingering. Hugs with Loraine were perfunctory. A necessary evil. A quick in and out without any emotion or warmth.

And Brian had wondered why she was in therapy twice a week.

Dr. Chandler wouldn't like this one bit. He'd ask why she was calling Loraine at all, what she hoped to achieve, why she kept searching for something that wasn't there, rather than just accepting it for what it was. Loraine wouldn't comfort her or tell her it would all be okay, or offer to make her tea the way Lindsay's mother would do. Yet for some reason, Kelly still held out hope that someday she would.

At times like this she was jealous of Hannah. And especially Evie. Other times, she just felt plain sorry for them. Her mother had left their father when Hannah was just a little girl and Evie was still a baby. Who was she to complain?

"I'm at the gym," Loraine replied, and crap, that was all it took. The "gym" was Kelly's magic word these days. The trigger that could shift her day from blue skies and sunshine to dark clouds and rain.

Unable to stop herself, she began to cry.

"Honey?" Okay, so maybe her mother wasn't so bad. She did call her "honey." On occasion. "Are you *crying*?"

Kelly pulled in a long, suffering breath that unfortunately sound like a long, dragged out snort. She cried harder just because of that.

"Did someone *die*?"

Kelly narrowed her eyes as the tears stopped. Her mother knew damn well that no one had died. Who was there to die? She had no extended family, other than her half-sisters, and her mother had an even more distant relationship with them than she did with the daughter she'd technically raised for eighteen years and then some, given that it wasn't until a year ago that Kelly could afford to get an apartment of her own. Damn you, San Francisco real estate!

"No," she said, bracing herself for what was about to come next.

"Well, *crying* doesn't solve anything. Are you at work? I hope you're not crying where people can see you!"

And there it was. The inevitable realization that she had made a fatal error in seeking comfort from the woman who gave her life and kept her alive until she was old enough to fend for herself. By Kelly's calculation, that was about seven years. By then she was pouring her own cereal for dinner on the nights her dad worked late, which was every night really, and putting herself to bed whenever she got tired.

"I should go," she said, wiping her eyes frantically. People were staring at her, sure, but did she care? No. She didn't. What she cared about was that her boyfriend was shagging Shannon and her boss had fired her and that her mother did not love her.

Well, she did love her. In her own special way.

"You'll get fired if you carry on this way at work. In my day, I wouldn't dare behave so emotionally in the office place!" Loraine scolded.

And in my day, I wouldn't ditch my two young daughters to start a new family, Kelly was tempted to snap back, but she refrained, because after all, if her mother hadn't left her first husband for Kelly's father, then what would she be? She wouldn't exist. She wouldn't be sitting here, in the middle of Union Square, crying over the mess her life had become.

Maybe that would have been better, actually.

She ended the call with barely a good-bye and stared miserably at her phone, willing it to light up with a text from Brian or an email from Hannah or, better yet, Evie. Surely Evie could ask Hannah for the email address, if she wanted to.

If she wanted to, Kelly thought sadly.

She should call Dr. Chandler, that's what she should really do, but then she remembered that he was on vacation. He spent two weeks of every September in Paris. She knew this because she'd been going to see him twice a week for forty-five minutes since she started college. Loraine had no idea. Loraine wouldn't approve. Loraine believed in holistic medicine. She'd tell Kelly to meditate or take a yoga class tonight.

But Kelly couldn't take a yoga class tonight because her yoga class was at the gym. And Brian was at the gym. With his hussy.

She whimpered so loudly that a dog lifting his leg at a nearby tree tilted his head to stare at her. She gave a watery smile in return until its owner hurried him away.

She stood up, deciding she would make her way home, figure out her life, or maybe just forget about it for a day, crawl into bed with a pint of ice cream instead. Normally, she took the trolley to and from the office, but today, she didn't dare part with the money. And so she walked, walked until her feet hurt and her heart was a little less heavy.

And today, like most other days, she wished that Hannah still lived in town. Only Hannah had ditched her...for her other sister.

Chapter Five

Hannah was looking at Evie with a critical eye. She hadn't said anything—yet—but she would, and soon. It would be tonight, because every other night since her first day at the paper, Evie had managed to dodge her sister by either going to bed early or pretending to be on the phone with an old friend from Boston who was having what she delicately referred to as a "life crisis."

Really, the person having the life crisis was her. She was now relying on cold showers and antihistamines to ward off hives. She couldn't lie in bed at night without her mind running through the path that had brought her to this point. A string of poor choices made with the best of intentions. She'd been the good girl, the conscientious daughter, dependable and responsible and diligent. She never missed a class, not even that one sophomore year of undergrad when she had a temperature of one hundred two and felt like she could nearly faint from fatigue. She was never late to anything, but always five minutes early. She was the best student in her graduating class at Oyster Bay High and maintained a solid GPA all through college. Her professors loved her. She was slated for big things.

And now she was hanging on to a job as a small-town newspaper columnist, and her boss was a man who, basically, didn't take her seriously enough to consider a real relationship with her!

And then there was the matter of the letter. Kelly's letter. The letter that still remained unopened. She'd transferred it from her handbag to her sock drawer, so she wouldn't be tempted to open it. Because she was tempted. A part of her longed to know what it said, to forge a connection with the sister she had never met, to understand what Hannah saw in her. To be included in the relationship they now had. But this was the part that stopped her every time. Made her stomach get that sick, hard feeling that she couldn't shake. Made her think of their childhood, and all those years that the mother she couldn't even remember had spent with another daughter, sometimes not even sending them a birthday or Christmas gift, much less show up for a dance recital or kiss them goodnight. And it made her think of Chip, how their father had done everything for them, desperate to make up for their mother's shortcomings, and how much she'd loved him for it and always would.

And how Hannah had still left. Left Chip and Evie behind to seek out Loraine. And Kelly.

And even though Hannah hadn't connected with their mother the way she had hoped, when Evie thought of her even trying, her heart hurt so badly that she wasn't sure she could forgive her sister for going out to California all those years ago, even though deep down a part of her could understand why Hannah did what she had. She needed something Evie that didn't. Evie was perfectly happy to surround herself with the family who stuck around. The ones who actually cared.

You can't make someone love you. That had been her motto, what she'd told herself every time she started to think of her mother.

Now, she applied that to a different person. A person she really needed to forget.

Evie took a long sip of her iced tea and leaned back in her chair. They were at Jojo's, just off Main, waiting for their cousin Abby to meet them for dinner, something that Evie had been looking forward to all week, only now that she was here she wished she was back in her room again, the door closed tight, topics she didn't want to discuss shut off.

She shifted her gaze away from her sister's, relief sweeping over her when she saw Abby approaching them on her vintage blue bicycle, her ponytail bouncing behind her. This was exactly what Evie needed. A distraction, and Abby was always good for it. She was happy to keep the conversation going in a positive direction, never one to broach uncomfortable topics, and always one for a good laugh. Recently, Evie had felt a little isolated when she got together with Hannah and Abby, who bonded over their reunited relationships with their old sweethearts and talked about the places they like to go on dates: Bistro del Mare for a special occasion, DiSotto's for pizza and beer after a long day at the beach, the Oyster Bay Hotel for a bottle of wine on the terrace. It reminded Evie that she couldn't really join in the conversation, that there was no one special in her past, and no one special in her present either. Occasionally she'd allow herself to imagine that what she had with Liam was more than it was. That it was special, meaningful, real. But even then, what could she say? They had actual boyfriends, and Evie had…well, a boss, as it turned out.

Tonight, however, she would be perfectly happy if Abby filled the entire meal with stories about Zach, and if Hannah went on and on about Dan and his daughter, Lucy, who Evie had to admit was a little sweetheart, and of course, really, she'd always liked Dan. She was happy for Hannah, genuinely happy, and she was even happier that Hannah had more reason to stay in Oyster Bay now that she and Dan were carrying on as if the decade she was gone had never happened.

Really, Hannah had everything and everyone she needed right here in this seaside town.

Well, everyone but Kelly…

"So!" Abby's eyes were wide as she pulled out her

chair and dropped into it. She was dressed in a bright green sundress covered by a well-worn jean jacket that Evie knew she had owned since high school and her cheeks had a natural glow. No doubt she would be stopping by to see Zach after this, just like Hannah would be off to see Dan. And Evie…Well, Evie planned to take a good book down to the beach to read, so long as there was ample light and the temperature didn't continue to drop. Already she'd had to put on a sweater with her jeans instead of the tee shirt she'd planned to wear. Autumn was fast approaching, and while the crisp air was something she usually welcomed, stirring up thoughts of freshly sharpened pencils and blank agendas just waiting to be filled and new possibilities, now it felt like an official good-bye to all those warmer nights and the way she'd spent them.

Evie expected Abby to give a juicy story about Zach or share some titillating piece of gossip from town. Instead, her cousin cocked her eyebrow suggestively and remarked, "I hear from Bridget that she has a dinner guest tonight."

Evie didn't need to ask what Abby was referring to. Jack and Liam had been friends back in New York, where Liam had been an editor for the publishing house that still published Jack's long-running series. Still, just the thought of Liam sitting in Bridget's dining room at the inn, or in the big kitchen that had once been the hub of the Harper family home and the home of many Christmas cookie baking sessions with dear Aunt Anne made Evie uncomfortable. That was her family. Her family's home, by extension. And Liam was encroaching on her personal turf.

That would be all fine and good—wonderful, really—if he hadn't been such a jerk about where things stood between them.

"So Jack's friend Liam has moved to Oyster Bay to run the paper? I heard it from Sarah first," Abby said as she slurped her glass of water.

Evie felt her temper rise. She couldn't help it. She liked Sarah, in fact, she considered her a good friend at this point. But the thought of Sarah even thinking about Liam was…well, it was…awful!

She took a sip from her own water glass, hoping to cool the heat that was building within her. "That's right," Evie managed, avoiding all eye contact with her sister. "He's the new boss!"

Abby just stared at her, clearly not buying her feigned nonchalance. "And you're trying to tell me that you're okay with that?"

Evie shrugged, but she struggled to maintain eye contact as she rearranged her fork and knife side by side.

With a lift of her eyebrows, Abby opened her menu and pretended to scan it, but Evie could tell that she was just stalling, hoping that by not looking interested, that Evie would break down and dish. Classic reverse psychology. Well, it wasn't going to work. Not on her.

She glanced at her sister, who remained equally silent.

Well, maybe it would.

"There's nothing going on between Liam and me," she said. Not anymore, at least.

Abby just jutted her lower lip and flipped to the next page in the menu, not even looking up. "If you say so."

"I do say so," Evie said firmly. Catching the amused look that passed between Hannah and Abby, she repeated herself, louder this time, unfortunately catching the attention of Dottie Joyce, the biggest busybody in town who had just taken the table three over and who now looked at her with keen interest. Damn it.

"Look," she said, lowering her voice to something just above a whisper. "There is nothing going on with Liam and me. I'm a professional, and he is my boss." And a real jerk, she thought.

Abby didn't look convinced but knew when to rest her case. Hannah, on the other hand, was looking at her very strangely. "And you're okay with that? Him just being your boss?"

Evie opened her menu. The words were a blur. "What we had was just…fun. Neither one of us is looking for anything serious."

And really, she wasn't. Or she hadn't been. Until…

"Evie!"

Evie turned to see Ron hurrying over to her, his grey tee shirt smeared with grease, a wild look in his eyes. From her periphery, she saw Abby poke Hannah. No one understood the patience she had for Ron.

"So you got the letters I sent you?"

Evie couldn't help but smile. She had responded to each and every one. "I did. *Don.*"

Rob grinned and looked around the table for approval. "Clever, eh?"

"Quite. Did you get my responses?" No doubt he had, but as to whether he had followed any of her advice, that was another matter.

"I did. But how come none of my letters have made the paper?"

"I have to give everyone a chance," she told him. She couldn't exactly harp on the same subject every day. Yesterday's column had gone to Bev. Today it had gone to a woman who was an only child dealing with an aging father and overbearing mother, and the conflicting feelings it stirred up. Evie assumed it was a letter from Courtney Jennings, whose father, Wally, had recently been diagnosed with early stages of dementia, and whose devotion to his wife Martha had earned him the nickname "Yes, Martha" around town.

"Tell you what? When you write to me about something other than your obsession with Jill, I will publish your letter."

"Obsession!" Ron looked stricken. "It's not an obsession!"

"It is an obsession, Ron," Evie said calmly. "Trailing your ex-wife in your car and calling her fifty-seven times in an hour is an obsession."

Hannah turned to her with wide eyes, but Evie didn't

react. Ron needed to be honest with himself and his actions if he was ever going to get on with his life and start feeling better. She would be doing him a disservice not to hold him accountable for his misery.

"But Jill's my wife!" Ron insisted.

Evie made an effort to keep her tone gentle yet firm. "Jill has filed for divorce. Jill wishes to move on, Ron. I think you should too."

"Harsh," Hannah hissed from behind her glass of wine.

Evie considered this. Yes, it was a bit frank, but what was the alternative? To tell Ron what he wanted to hear? He was seeking her help, and that's what she was offering.

"I'll work on a new letter," Ron said, nodding slowly. "I'll go do that right now."

It was Thursday evening and Ron was off work for the day. Evie wanted to tell him to go out, have a beer and a burger, but then she considered that staying home writing her a letter at least kept him from stalking Jill.

"You do that, Ron. And it was good seeing you!"

Evie turned back to Hannah, smiling, because it *had* been good to see Ron. He'd made her time tending bar downright enjoyable, taken away the disappointment she'd felt that she was pouring drinks instead of doing what she'd sought out to do. But then Ron came in, with his broken heart, and she'd been able to help him. Someday she'd let him know just how much he helped her too. But not yet. Not until he was in a new phase of life.

She sipped her water and looked up at her sister and cousin, who were now looking at her as if she had two heads. "What?"

"I didn't say a word," Hannah replied and reached her glass.

"No, but you were thinking it." Evie looked from Hannah to Abby, who was equally quiet. "Go on, what is it?"

"I'm just thinking about what you said to Ron." She hesitated, as if not sure she should continue.

"And?" Evie said loudly, again piquing Dottie's interest.

"Well, it really is hard to get over someone that you were in love with. It's not as simple as just moving on," Hannah said.

Evie blinked at her sister in disbelief. "I never said it was simple!" She felt angry, emotional even, and she realized with a start that she wasn't even thinking of Ron and Jill at all. She was thinking of herself. And Liam.

Abby said, "Maybe you should tell him to volunteer for Fall Fest!"

"Are you entering your pie again this year?" Hannah asked. Abby let everyone she knew know that she had been runner up in last year's contest.

"No, no, this year I'm just a spectator. It will be a busy weekend at the inn, with guests coming in for the event."

"You should sign up to volunteer, Evie," Hannah said.

"Sarah's signing up and she asked me, but it's not really my thing."

It wasn't Evie's thing either, but that didn't mean it would stop her.

Sure she'd sign up for the Fall Fest committee. Do exactly as she had advised Ron. It would keep her busy and with any luck, it might just take her mind off Liam and those magical summer nights that had somehow, all too harshly, cooled with the change of season.

*

Liam accepted the beer that Jack handed him and followed his friend out onto the back deck of the old seaside Victorian house where Jack had been married and now lived with Bridget and her daughter, Emma. "Only until the carriage house renovation is finished," Jack clarified. The house had been transformed into an inn last fall and the living quarters were small and currently just off the kitchen. Jack explained that they would repurpose those rooms into two more suites, since, most of the time, and especially in summer, they had no vacancy and had to turn people away.

"Could be worse!" Jack said with a happy shrug. "And the carriage house is the perfect solution."

He led Liam over to it now, crossing the white-painted porch that gave a never-ending view of the Atlantic dotted with white sails from bobbing boats, and across the gravel driveway to the cedar-sided outparcel that was slowly being transformed. There was a gleam in Jack's eye as he led Liam through the construction site and pointed out where rooms would go, finally referring to a blueprint that was spread out on a card table in the center of the main living space.

Liam nodded politely and said all the right things, but inside, the demon was growing bigger, just as it always did at times like this, when he was reminded of what he once had, and lost. When he saw someone else moving forward, and all he could do was move backward in return.

After all, he'd been here once. Had this moment. When they were first engaged, Ellen and he had gone apartment hunting, narrowing their search to the Upper West Side, so they had easy access to Central Park and a short commute to their Midtown offices. Most of the places they looked at were shockingly bad, some with a bathtub in the kitchen, some with no bathtub at all. Some had no fridge. Others had no oven. But Ellen didn't give up. It was a hunt, she said, and oh, did she enjoy it. So much, in fact, that she often said she wouldn't know what to do when they finally settled down. Maybe she was meant to be a real estate agent instead of a gallery assistant.

When they finally found something—a rare gem they'd outbid three other couples for and celebrated with a bottle of cheap champagne, since they had little left for extravagances now—she'd spent weekends fixing it up, framing photos of them on their wedding day, their honeymoon, their first Christmas…

And their last Christmas.

His jaw set just thinking about it, and he took another sip of his beer, telling himself he should really slow down if he was going to drive and then remembering that he had walked here. The house wasn't too far from town, where he was renting a two-bedroom apartment near the library, and besides, he was used to walking. He walked everywhere in New York.

"You ever miss it?" he asked Jack, as they made their way back to the main house, an old, seafront Victorian that had supposedly been in the Harper family for generations. There were guests, but the ones he had seen since arriving kept to themselves, either letting themselves in the front door to climb the stairs to their room or sitting in the lobby, quietly reading. Now a couple was on the back porch, sharing a bottle of wine at one of the café tables, their faces positioned toward the ocean. The woman's dark hair blew in the breeze, and that one small trigger was all it took for Liam to flash back to the night he'd proposed to Ellen, out in the Hamptons, when they were staying at an inn just like this, with the view of the same body of water.

"I don't miss it, believe it or not," Jack was saying, and Liam forced himself back to the present. Pushed the ache that had crept into his chest away. He wanted to forget her nearly as much as he wanted to cling to her. He didn't know which was worse some days.

"What about you?" Jack asked as he dropped onto a

chair at the far end of the patio.

Liam took a seat with his back to the couple and the woman with the dark hair. He considered the question for a moment, and finally shrugged. "Jury's still out."

Jack's face turned serious for a moment and Liam wished he'd just lied through his teeth, told his buddy what he wanted to hear—what everyone wanted to hear! That he was great, wonderful, never better. That he didn't spend half his days living with guilt and the other half living with dread. That he didn't know how to move on, and he wasn't even sure he wanted to. That most nights when he closed his eyes, he heard the brake of the tires, the scream beside him. He'd climbed out of the car with a broken thumb. A thumb!

But more had broken than just that thumb that day. His heart had broken the moment he looked over and saw Ellen's lifeless body, when the horrible sensation that he couldn't turn back time no matter how much he wanted to took hold and never let go again.

"You did the right thing coming here," Jack said firmly, and Liam nodded, wanting to believe his friend was right, but feeling lost all the same. Coming here felt like giving up, closing a door on the life he'd had, even if he had to admit that part of it felt like a relief.

Here, in Oyster Bay, there were no reminders of Ellen. He didn't have to look into the kitchen and imagine her standing there, pouring coffee, still wearing her pink striped pajama pants. He didn't have to crawl into his bed and stare at the wood dresser that still housed her clothes. He didn't have to think about what to do with them, knowing that enough time had passed that it was technically acceptable to donate them.

Everything from the apartment had gone into storage. He hadn't shared that and he didn't plan to. Jack, like everyone else, had the best intentions. But he didn't understand. No one could.

"It's a nice community," Jack continued, as if sensing that Liam wasn't completely embracing this new change. "And you know some people, right? Bridget's cousin, Evie?"

Liam looked at Jack sharply. He'd suspected that Jack was aware of what had transpired with Evie over the summer. After all, some of their flirtation had happened right here, on this property, and with Bridget being Evie's cousin, it was more than likely that word would travel. Still, Jack had never said anything. Had maybe known better. Until now.

"Yeah, I know Evie," Liam said, trying to keep his tone casual.

"Pretty girl," Jack said. "Smart too. And sweet. Evie's a good egg."

Liam narrowed his eye at his friend. Was Jack trying to sell him on Evie or warn him? He couldn't be sure. Either way, he needed to put this topic to rest. "Evie works at the paper. I'm her boss."

"So?" Jack shot back.

Liam felt a stir of impatience. "So, that's a conflict of

interest."

"So, quit." Jack shrugged, as if it were just that simple, as if Liam's new job was the only thing keeping him from living happily ever after.

Didn't Jack know by now that Liam didn't believe in that crap?

"I'm not quitting my job," Liam said clearly. "And I'm not getting involved with Evie either. She's a nice girl, as you said, and she deserves more than I can give her."

Jack shook his head, seeming frustrated, but said nothing more.

The back door opened and Bridget stepped through, an apron tied around her waist was smeared with pasta sauce. "Dinner should be ready soon." She shivered as she looked out onto the lawn and rubbed her bare arms. "Fall is coming." She grinned. "Wait until you guys see fall in Oyster Bay. People go all out with the pumpkins and scarecrows. I'm thinking I'll do a different theme each year for the inn. They even offer a decorating contest at the Fall Fest. I assume that you will be coming to the annual Fall Fest?"

Jack gave Liam a rueful look. "She dragged me to the *Flower* Fest when I first came here."

"And aren't you glad I did?" Bridget nudged his shoulder with her hip and tousled his hair fondly. Liam couldn't help it. It hurt him to watch.

He looked down at his beer. The foam had settled and the glass was warm to the touch from gripping the bottle so tight.

"I was just telling Liam that he did the right thing getting out of the city. If you start talking about Flower Fests and Pumpkin Fests—"

"*Fall* Fest," Bridget corrected. Liam grinned.

"Fall Fest," Jack repeated. "You know you're going to drive him out of town."

"Actually, I think these festivals are a great way to get involved," Bridget said. She was staring at Liam in a way that made him uneasy, as if she had plans for him, plans he didn't have for himself, only at least her ideas were more harmless than the ones he'd heard in the past. Usually it was that someone knew the perfect girl to set him up with, and no amount of polite protests would make them back down, until he resorted to getting firm, his tone more forceful than he wished it needed to be.

Everyone knew what was best for him. And he didn't know what was best anymore.

Still, maybe they were right, about coming here at least. It felt better—if not a little strange—to come home to his new surroundings each night and wake up to a new bedroom every morning. Here in Oyster Bay, there were no memories at every turn. If he allowed himself to, he could almost start to believe that the life he'd shared with Ellen never existed.

But he couldn't do that. Didn't want to do that.

"If you're sticking around you may as well meet some people," Jack encouraged. "Friends, nothing more." He held up his hands, in a truce perhaps to show that he was backing off on the subject of Evie.

Jack and Bridget had a good point, and meeting new people, people who didn't know about his past and therefore couldn't comment on it…that was almost as appealing as the thought of not going home to that empty apartment, even if it was empty by choice.

"Sign me up," he said with a grin.

Chapter Six

The next morning, Evie slid into work fifteen minutes before the office officially opened, when only Sarah was already there, brewing the coffee.

"You're here early!" Sarah remarked as she filled her mug.

"You know me. I'm overly conscientious," Evie said. That was the term she'd heard all through school, right up until that disastrous interview at the hospital in Boston last spring. She worked too hard. Tried too hard. She was too focused. She hadn't even known such a thing was possible, let alone that she would be punished for it!

"Trying to impress the big boss, eh?" Sarah gave her a little smile as she tapped her spoon against the rim of her mug. "I figured he'd go easy on you, seeing that you guys were friendly."

Friendly was hardly the way Evie would describe it. "Actually, if anything, I think he'd be harder on me," she said, reaching for a paper cup.

"Because of perceived favoritism?" Sarah asked.

Or because he didn't want to send her the wrong message. Lead her on. Make her think he was interested when he so clearly wasn't.

Evie shrugged to dismiss the question and poured herself a cup of coffee, knowing it might be the only one she got for the day, considering the kitchen was two doors down from Liam's office and therefore in the danger zone, and carried it back to her cubicle, where she happily hid behind her computer screen. A new set of emails had arrived from readers needing help, and, for a moment, her own troubles were lost as she engrossed herself in the trials of her fellow Oyster Bay residents, because contrary to what Liam might aspire to, the only people who read the daily rag, even the online version, which was already up and running as promised, were the locals.

Evie sipped her coffee as she read the first letter and sent a reply. She checked the clock at the bottom right corner of her screen, seeing that only twenty minutes had passed, and picked up her cup of coffee, allowing herself a quick glance around the office. Liam's office was shut, the lights out. Hannah's cube was vacant, she was probably out on a photo shoot—she'd mentioned something last night about an upcoming article on the plans to revitalize Main Street next spring. She could maybe pop up and grab another cup of coffee if she was quick, but…

And here he came.

Her breath caught as she looked down at her keyboard, her hands now shaking so hard that she was happy she hadn't bothered to refill that coffee, she only would have sloshed it all over her clothes. He was on his cell phone, and she wondered who he could be talking to, wondering if it was a girlfriend, if that was why he couldn't have something serious with her, if he had already moved on. He was distracted, frowning a bit, allowing her a good long look in his direction, at his neatly trimmed brown hair and those warm, chocolate eyes, and the crisp white shirt and charcoal suit that was completely out of place in Oyster Bay but that made her love him all the more.

No, not love. Definitely not love. She was not in love with Liam! She couldn't be.

This was her sign. She didn't usually believe in such nonsense, but this situation called for extreme measures. The man that she had spent night after night with, the man who had made her finally understand what everyone meant when they said they were "smitten," the man who filled her dreams long after he had left to go back to New York, was her boss. And she didn't date bosses. And he had no interest in dating her anyway.

Right. She pulled up the Internet and logged into the job posting board that was linked to her old university, relieved that she still had access, even if she had officially received her degree last spring.

There were few postings, some that she wasn't qualified for, others that she was over qualified for. Some were in places like New York, Seattle, and Chicago. She flagged the few that looked like possibilities, even if her heart no longer felt in it. She'd made peace with staying in Oyster Bay, even dared to think that she would be happy writing an advice column for the local paper, helping the fellow members of the community she'd grown up in.

But now Liam was here. And everything was different. She was being forced to make a change. Maybe forced to realize that this wasn't where she was meant to be at all.

With new determination, she pulled up her personal email account, found a copy of her resume in the attachment she'd first sent to Jim, and opened it. Of course, there was nothing to update, but still she skimmed it, reviewing her list of accomplishments, her grade point average, a few academic awards she'd even earned over the years. How could it have not been enough?

Heart sinking, she considered not even bothering, just giving up. She'd go back to The Lantern, ask her father to take pity on her, give her back the bartending gig. She'd be a lifer like Joann. It wouldn't be so bad.

Actually, it would. Her father loved the restaurant scene, and yes, she did enjoy helping out, but it wasn't her calling. It wasn't living up to her potential.

She stared at the resume, willing it to be enough this

time. Maybe this time the universe would take pity on her. Maybe this time something would work out in her favor.

"What are you doing?" a voice behind her came from nowhere.

Evie jumped, clicking out of the document as quickly as her trembling fingers would let her, only to process that it was just Sarah, who was looking at her with a frown.

"Just um…" Evie shook her head. She couldn't lie to her friend, and she couldn't think of an excuse fast enough. Instead she said, "Abby mentioned that you're going to the festival planning committee. I think I'll join you."

Join. When was the last time she'd joined anything? That was the one thing missing from her resume. The one key that might unlock the door to new opportunities.

"I'm hoping there are some cute guys there," Sarah said, but from the look on her face, it was clear she'd prepared herself for this not to be the case.

"Men are just trouble," Evie grumbled.

Sarah looked at her suspiciously. "I thought you said nothing happened between you and Liam."

"Who said I was talking about Liam?" Evie said, jutting her chin and turning back to her computer. Why couldn't Ron email her now? Or Bev again? She needed an excuse to get back to work.

"If you say so," Sarah said, a little smile forming on her lips. Evie wasn't quite sure what it was all about, but she didn't want to ask. So maybe Sarah liked Liam. Why shouldn't she? He was tall and handsome and…right there.

He was walking down the hall, a cup of coffee in his hand, and for a moment both Evie and Sarah followed his path. Finally, his door closed, and Sarah looked down at Evie, the grin broader now. "There's hope for Oyster Bay yet. See you tomorrow at Town Hall!"

As soon as Sarah walked away, Evie pulled back up her document added a new section to her resume, titled "Committees." So what if she was jumping the gun? As of tomorrow, it would be legitimate. And so with that, she saved the resume and sent it off to five job postings, and then crossed every finger and toe.

She was going to get out of this town. She was going to get away from Liam. And she was going to be okay. Somehow.

*

By six thirty on Friday evening, Kelly was ashamed to admit that since losing her job she had enjoyed three cartons of ice cream (mint chocolate chip, cookies and cream, and peanut butter cup), an entire roll of raw cookie dough, six bottles of wine, and four frozen pizzas. She felt wretched. Normally, she existed on green smoothies and kale salads with a lean protein, but what did it matter anymore? She couldn't go to the gym without feeling like she could die, and she really did hate running and really couldn't be bothered, especially since there was no point to any of it. What did any of it matter? Had that tight butt and nicely brushed hair kept her boyfriend from wandering to her friend? Had her crisp wardrobe helped her keep her job?

She was now living in the college sweatpants she'd forgotten she owned. She did shower (she wasn't that sad a case—yet) but she slid back into the same pants after each rinse, and then slid right back onto her favorite position on the couch, the remote control within reach.

But now she was out of wine and pizza and ice cream and her stomach sort of hurt and she was craving some normalcy, like…a piece of fruit or something that didn't come out of a box.

With a sigh, she knew she had no choice but to drag herself from the pile of throw pillows that propped her up, and walk to the store for supplies. She pulled her hair back into a ponytail and exchanged the sweats for her jeans, a little startled at how tight they already felt, and tossed a jacket and scarf over the pink Henley she'd also been wearing for more days than she could count.

She'd buy eggs. And milk. And fruit. She would not walk into the frozen section. She wouldn't even consider the extensive variety of ice cream flavors that made her salivate. She would certainly not even look at the rack of frozen pizzas. Even the veggie ones.

She was going to cleanse. Her body. Her spirit. She would exorcise the negativity from her life and then find a renewed energy and sense of purpose. Yes!

The temperature had dropped since the last time she'd

been outside, the morning of her…turning point. Yes, that's what she'd call it. The day she said good-bye to the job she'd never even liked in the first place, other than the fact that it had afforded her the opportunity to move out of her parents' house and into a place of her own. Really, the work had been trying, boring and taxing. When she complained to her father he looked at her quizzically and said, "Welcome to the real world, Kelly!" in a way that really wasn't very inviting at all and made her wonder just how her parents had ever connected, much less stuck it out as long as they had.

But then, of course, her father traveled, and Loraine was busy with her own thing, like yoga at her gym, and she liked the freedom that came with money. She often snorted in reference to her first husband, Chip Donovan, Hannah and Kelly's father, who was a restaurant owner in a small town in Maine, a far cry from the laid-back sophistication of San Francisco, Kelly supposed.

Her mother wouldn't have wanted her to sell out, of this she was sure. When Kelly had taken the job at the real estate firm, Loraine had given her a strange look, but said nothing. She was good at keeping her thoughts to herself like that, but still Kelly sensed her mother's disappointment, always had. She remembered in that moment asking what was so wrong with following a corporate path. After all, Chip had followed his heart, and that hadn't met Loraine's approval either! Sometimes Kelly couldn't help wondering if anything ever would.

The store was up ahead now and Kelly walked through the electronic doors and grabbed a basket. She took her usual route, starting with the produce and working her way over to dairy. She studiously ignored the frozen section, as well as the spirits aisle, and felt immensely proud of herself for selecting some lentils and quinoa for easy meals rather than the processed junk that no doubt tasted better. It was all about taking back the control. She'd let too many others control her emotions for far too long and look where it had gotten her.

My, wouldn't Dr. Chandler be proud! Well, maybe not about the being fired bit, but she'd gloss over that part.

"I love your scarf," a woman holding a drooling baby on her hip said as Kelly leaned over a bushel of apples to bag a few.

She smiled and touched the mohair fabric that was wrapped around her neck. "Thank you. I knitted it."

The woman's eyes rounded with surprise. "You *made* that?"

Kelly hadn't thought much of it until now. It was just a hobby, something she'd picked up in high school and rarely had time for these days. Still, it cheered her up, made her happy she had forced herself off the couch and out of the apartment. Smiling, she walked over to the bakery section, just for a look, not a buy, and nearly collided with Shannon.

She blinked, her mind on overdrive as she contemplated how to handle this situation. How to avoid it. She wanted to run. Drop her basket and sprint all the way home. But she couldn't. And so, in an attempt to pick up what was left of her dignity, she feigned nonchalance.

"Hi, Shannon," she said casually, transferring the basket from her left wrist to her right.

"Hi, Kelly," Shannon said, looking almost more alarmed than Kelly felt. "I…wasn't sure you'd say hello to me."

"And why wouldn't I say hello to you?" Kelly asked, knowing she was putting Shannon on the spot and wondering if it would force an apology. She deserved one.

"Oh, you know, because of what happened, with you and Brian breaking up." Shannon chewed her bottom lip. A habit that Kelly had always found irritating but that Brian probably found cute.

Technically, they hadn't broken up, Kelly wanted to point out. A break up, in Kelly's opinion, was a mutual agreement. Two individuals weren't getting along. It was time to part ways. Not the case in her situation. She was in love with Brian. She'd thought he loved her too. But it turned out he loved Shannon. It would be a perfect love triangle aside from the fact that Shannon loved him as well.

"Oh, well, I'm better off without him," Kelly blurted. Her heart was pounding in her chest now and she felt nearly delirious from the exhilaration of saying that out loud. She was better off without him, the cheating louse! The man had played her. Strung her along and messed with her heart. Was this the kind of man who deserved her love and respect? Absolutely not.

"I can tell you're still upset," Shannon said gently. "We didn't ever want to hurt you, Kelly."

"Hurt me?" Now Kelly was getting mad. Is this what they thought? That they had hurt her? Of course they had, and badly, but she wouldn't show it.

"Well, I mean, you haven't been around the gym lately—"

"I've been running. Fresh air. Training for the marathon actually." It was such a bold-faced lie that she wondered if Shannon would even believe her. It would be a real test of their friendship, she supposed, to see how well Shannon knew her.

But then, Shannon had already failed the friendship test, hadn't she?

"Wow! I'm…impressed." Shannon still looked hesitant and Kelly felt the need to end this conversation once and for all.

"Honestly, I'm fine. Relieved, really. Brian and I weren't a fit. The two of you are a far better match." Both devoid of loyalty, she thought. No doubt they would cheat on each other within the next three months. They had it coming.

Now Shannon had the nerve to grin. "Brian and I said the exact same thing!"

And it was officially time to leave. "Well, I'd better go," she said, scooting past Shannon, eager to get out of the store and home to her tiny, cramped, impossibly empty apartment. "Nice seeing you, Shannon. And...good luck."

Shannon frowned at this, and Kelly left her to process what she meant by that. She lifted her chin and walked out of the produce section, toward the processed junk, which she would be loading up on, oh yes. She turned to go down the crackers and cookies row when she dared to turn her head, for one last look, and there he was. Brian. Her Brian, up until a few weeks ago. She didn't know why she hadn't expected him to be here. It was Friday night. Shannon and Brian were dating. They were probably picking up food for a cozy dinner at home, after which they'd retire to Brian's bed and...

She turned down the aisle of the frozen section. To hell with her good intentions! As quickly as she could, she loaded up her basket with ice cream and frozen pizza and even microwaveable pretzels stuffed with cheese. Jalapeno poppers. Some sorbet to cleanse her pallet.

So she was going to eat her emotions. She had to do something. And right now, she could do nothing, nothing but think about how handsome Brian still looked in that hunter green sweater and those jeans that were fading at the knee and that she knew from experience were so soft that he said he'd never get rid of them, even once they finally ripped from wear.

She moved to the front of the store, barely daring to breathe, and waited behind a rack of flowers for Brian and Shannon to check out, noticing every item they pulled from their basket. Wine. Cheese. Bread. Some grapes. Honestly, could they be any more of a cliché? No doubt this was Shannon's idea for a cute date.

A date that Kelly pathetically wished she had planned herself back when Brian was still with her.

She waited until they left and then brought her basket to the cashier, hoping that her ice cream hadn't melted but almost not even caring. Her appetite was lost, and her heart felt heavy with dread again.

She wanted to call Dr. Chandler. But he was in Paris. She wanted to call Hannah, but she was in Maine now, back to her old life.

She could call Lindsay from work, suggest they meet up for drinks, but she didn't want to be reminded of the job she'd lost, and how the world seemed to be going on for everyone else around her.

She walked home slowly, stopping at the mailbox to confirm what she already knew, that Evie hadn't written back yet, that her letter hadn't gotten her attention. That she didn't want to have a relationship and why, Kelly couldn't understand. All Hannah had ever said was that Evie didn't support her going out to California, that Evie had hard feelings toward their mother, that she dealt with it differently.

But Kelly wasn't Loraine! Far from it!

She trudged up the stairs to her apartment door. The walk felt longer than ever, no doubt because of the extra weight she'd slapped on over the past few days. She put the food in the freezer and set the timer on the oven for the frozen pizza.

She stared at the laptop, knowing she should sit down, start a resume, and definitely not look up Brian's profile on Facebook and see how his little wine and cheese date was going tonight.

Instead, she opened the laptop and typed in her sister's name. Evie Donovan. Instantly, a link came up for the *Oyster Bay Gazette*, something that hadn't been there just a week ago when she'd done the same search, desperate for connection with the woman who remained such a mystery.

She clicked on the link, scanning the page until she came to the Ask Evie column. There was a picture of her sister, a new one, probably taken within the past few weeks. She was wearing glasses, looking extremely studious and knowledgeable, but there was a faint smile on her lips, one that couldn't help but make Kelly feel (despite the glaring lack of communication) that Evie was, in fact, quite approachable.

She read her sister's column, devouring every word and then starting at the beginning again once she'd reached the end. And then, there at the bottom, she saw the button. "Do you have a problem that you'd like to ask Evie?"

She did! She did have a problem! Many, in fact. So many that she didn't know where to begin. And her sister—her actual sister—was going to be the one to help her!

She nearly wept for joy.

Chapter Seven

Liam looked around the small apartment that was now, technically, his home, and wondered for the umpteenth time if he had made a colossal mistake. When Jack had first made the introduction to Jim Stafford, with the gentle and clearly premeditated suggestion that the two men talk, considering they had a lot in common, Liam saw the opportunity to take over this small-town paper as a relief. Gone would be the days of working for fifteen hours at the publishing house, staying long after the clean-up crew had come through, prolonging the inevitable return to a dark apartment. He'd walk home, even in the rain, instead of taking the subway, relishing in the noise and the distraction that Manhattan could bring, his heart growing heavy with dread when he rounded Seventy-Second Street and saw the brownstone up ahead, remembering when he and Ellen had first seen it, up ahead, how she'd grabbed his arm excitedly and pointed out the window boxes and told him that this one was it, she was sure of it.

He'd been skeptical, said they hadn't even been inside yet, asked how she could know.

"Some things just feel right," she'd told him.

And Oyster Bay…it had felt right. Just like that brownstone apartment that now belonged to two college grads who would have no idea how much love had been made and lost in those four walls. How his wife had spent three weeks trying out paint samples before finalizing the perfect shade of beige.

How that apartment had been filled with laughter and joy and, later, sorrow and anger.

They'd never know. And now, this new home, if he could call it that, was filled with nothing. Not a photo on the wall. Not a scratch on the woodwork. Not a memory to be shared or clung to.

He didn't know which was worse.

Manhattan, he decided. His life there was dark and unhappy and full of ghosts he couldn't get away from. And Oyster Bay had felt right. The sea breeze, the salty air, the sunshine, and a friend in place. He'd taken the job without much of a pause, anticipating his new life here as the escape that it was meant to be.

And then he'd met Evie. Or seen her. Hobbling around at the rehearsal dinner on the eve of Jack's wedding, he'd assumed she was two sheets to the wind, and he'd had a few drinks himself. Weddings brought out the worst in him, reminded him of what he'd had, and lost. So he'd had a few beers, numbed the pain a bit, and sought out what he usually did: a distraction.

That was all Evie was ever meant to be. And yet...

Some things just feel right. If he closed his eyes, he could see Ellen's smile as she said that, leading him by the hand, eager to get started on the next phase of their life.

Liam stood, grabbed his laptop and shoved it into a fading navy backpack he'd had since college. It was frayed and loose but comfortable, a part of the past that didn't fill him with bad memories.

He walked the few short blocks into town, which was mostly comprised of one long street that hugged the shoreline, filled with shops and restaurants whose doors were flanked by urns of flowers in bright colors. The sidewalks were filled, a busy Saturday afternoon, and he pushed through the door of Angie's, a café he'd been to nearly every day since first visiting town, hoping to snag a table and not have to order something to go. The owner was usually back in the kitchen, and today a girl who appeared to be in high school filled his mug and added a complimentary chocolate chip cookie, something that would never have happened back in Manhattan.

Here in Oyster Bay, people knew how you took your coffee. They knew where you worked. They knew anything about you that you were willing to share, or let slip, which was why Liam was grateful that Jack and his new wife were able to be discreet. If word got out that the new head of the newspaper was a widower, he'd be getting pitying glances for the rest of his days here, which would be limited, that much was for sure.

He sipped his coffee and pulled up his email, managing a smile at the older women sitting in the corner opposite him, who giggled in response and went back to their whispering. *Don't even think about it*, he wanted to say. He'd heard all about how some of the women in town could be, eager to set up their children or grandchildren and see them settled. In fact, Evie had touched upon such a subject matter in her column earlier in the week, one that had made him laugh out loud, after hours in his office, when he was putting the issue to bed.

Curious, he pulled up his email and scanned the inbox for Evie's newest column, scheduled for tomorrow's edition. Technically, as her boss, he could give her editorial notes before passing anything through to print tonight, but her insight was always spot on, better than he could offer, and he found himself drawn to her approach to people's problems.

He read the column with interest, about a woman whose boyfriend left her for her friend, and who was so upset by the break up that she'd stopped going anywhere he went, including her favorite places, and had lost her job from poor performance.

As usual, Evie's response was what one might classify as tough love.

Dear Lost,

Contrary to what you think, you have not lost anything. Rather, you have chosen to give away what you have earned and enjoyed to a person who, if you are being honest with yourself, is undeserving of such generosity! You did not lose your boyfriend. He chose, instead, to leave. Ditto for the so-called friend. You cannot hold onto what was never yours. But you should absolutely hold onto what is rightfully yours! It is time to go back to the gym, and the grocery store, and reclaim your life. If anyone should be hiding, it is those who wronged you! So lift your chin! Brush your hair and get outside. And if all else fails, knit.

Liam smiled, he couldn't help it. Knitting was something she'd advised another person to do, and he wondered if it worked, and he also wondered if Evie knitted in her spare time. She hadn't mentioned it in all those days they'd spent together, but then, she hadn't mentioned a lot of things, like where her easy listening skills came from, and why she was pouring drinks instead of pursuing her practice.

Why *had* she been working at The Lantern? It was her father's restaurant, he knew that much, and he supposed it made sense that she put in a few hours there while she was job searching. Maybe there was nothing more to it than that.

He signed off on the article and leaned back in his chair, realizing that by now his coffee had grown cold. He couldn't help it, he wanted to talk to her, wanted to go back to those summer nights where they could talk about anything, well, almost anything. Back to a time when he actually felt like for once he might be able to get close, open up, share. But then, it was time to go. His two weeks in town were up. He'd left, feeling a bit relieved actually, knowing that his secret was still intact, that his past was still preserved, that he hadn't allowed himself to cross that line that he had created the day that Ellen had passed and his life had changed forever.

He'd kept Evie, like all the others, at a safe distance. But now, there was no running back to New York. There was no easy excuse. And he longed for those conversations and the way he felt when he was with her all those evenings.

And he longed for her to tell him what to do, what to think, what to say. Because he didn't know what he was doing anymore. He hadn't in a long time.

He took a sip of his lukewarm coffee and opened a fresh page in his word processor. Maybe he was crossing a line, or maybe he was trying to connect with Evie in a way that he no longer could, face to face, or maybe, just maybe, he was finally seeking the help he needed.

He paused, but only for a moment. He'd worry about all that later.

For now, he'd chalk it up to giving Evie more material for her article. After all, he had a paper to run and readership to grow. He'd support the cause, and maybe, find a little something extra along the way…

*

Evie met Sarah at six sharp, wishing she was home

with a good book, or better yet, on the beach. October was just around the corner and there wouldn't be many warm days left, not that she particularly minded. She'd always loved Maine in the fall, felt more relaxed and in her element in a thick sweater, with an excuse to stay indoors instead of outside, participating in all the events that others so naturally found amusing.

Sure enough, Sarah dragged out a sigh as they walked up the steps of Town Hall for the Fall Fest planning committee meeting, pointing to her jeans and heather grey sweater. "I can't believe that summer is over. All those wonderful days down at the beach. All those wonderful seasonal employees at the restaurants…"

"You mean all those hot seasonal employees," Evie said with a grin.

Sarah glanced at her. "They were a bit young," she admitted.

"You think?" Evie hooted. Her college years were long behind her. She wasn't looking for the young, sporty, overly tanned guys who were headed back to Tufts or Harvard or Penn in September. She was looking for…

Liam.

Her eyes narrowed on the familiar figure at the front of the room, listening patiently to Beverly Wright, who seemed quite agitated if her body language said anything. Both hands were resting firmly on her hips and her mouth was moving so quickly that Evie had to think that for once, she was talking about something other than her desire to find poor Tim a match.

Not wanting to engage with either party at the moment, Evie tried to steer Sarah toward the refreshment table, compliments of Angie's, but it was no use. Sarah had spotted Liam and now her expression had completely transformed.

"Well, look who's here." She gave Evie the side eye. Evie pretended not to see.

Instead she took extreme interest in surveying the cookie tray, and there was quite a variety: lemon bars, three kinds of brownies, at least six different kinds of cookies, from chocolate chip to sugar butter. No doubt Abby would roll her eyes at this. Ever since her cousin took over the kitchen at the inn, she felt a sense of competition with Angie, who used to cater the inn's breakfasts with her pastries.

"I would think that Liam would be too cool for a small-town party planning committee," Sarah said, studying him across the room.

Evie tried to distract her by offering her a double chocolate fudge cookie, but Sarah all but swatted it away.

"Why?" Evie said, leaning back against the table to reflect on the man who was, yes, quite cool, at least if the dark jeans, camel Henley, and the backpack slung over his shoulder said anything.

"Well, he just moved here from New York City!" Sarah said this as if this should be obvious.

"So, I just moved back here from Boston," Evie pointed out, but Sarah just gave her a funny look and then squeezed her elbow.

"Oh, I know, but…"

Evie got it. Of course. She was quiet and reserved and maybe even a little nerdy, at least according to her high school classmates. Whereas Liam was tall and handsome and exuded self-confidence and a certain air of inapproachability, until you got to know him, and you learned that he was actually not just friendly, but very sweet, too.

He'd made her feel comfortable, special even, and sure, she had swapped out her glasses for contacts and swiped on a little lipstick for effort, but she was still the same shy girl who hidden in the bathroom for school dances and hadn't had her first kiss until she was nineteen, something that no one else knew, despite their suspicions, no doubt. He'd brought baskets of food for picnics on the beach, bringing a bottle of red and a bottle of white on the first night, because he didn't know which she preferred. And when he learned that she had a weakness for the chocolate-covered blueberries that only came out in the summer, he'd made a point to bring some the next time he saw her. He was thoughtful. Kind. And…warm.

Now, looking at him from this distance, Evie felt like she was looking at a stranger, not someone who'd been, well, so much more than that.

She grabbed a plate and loaded it with cookies, a brownie, and a lemon bar, ignoring Sarah's wide-eyed stare. So this was what she had been missing out on all those years when she was busy cramming for a possible pop test or working on extra credit projects. Clubs and committees offered food. Lots of it. And free, too. The best kind.

"What are you going to sign up for?" Sarah asked as they moved toward the first table. The room was filled with card tables, each with its own topic and sign-up sheet. There were the food trucks and the games and the decorating committee, which always filled up fast, she'd overheard, and the music and entertainment section. There was even a sign-up sheet for security, in case things got a little too rowdy, like the time that Dottie insisted they have a tug of rope with a big, wet, mud pit, men versus women. It was right after her husband left her, and she was feeling angry.

Sarah shuddered when she saw what the next sheet was for: the kiddie carnival, which usually meant free babysitting due to the parents who left their kids there in search of a few minutes of adult fun at the cider stand. "I got stuck manning the kids at the last festival. I can promise you, if I close my eyes, I can still see little Delia Walker's tonsils when she didn't earn a prize in the ring toss."

Evie laughed. "She is a screamer. Her parents came into The Lantern one night when I was working and she practically had to be dragged off the floor when we ran out of coloring sheets." Evie smiled when she thought of the look in Chip's eyes. She half expected him to pull up a seat at the bar, order a tall one, and unload on her the way all the others did. Over time, she'd come to know them all, not just by name, but by life crisis: broken hearts were the most common, but of course there were the financial woes, the bad boss complaints, and the family dramas. That day, Chip's life crisis was overworked single father with two grown daughters still mooching off him for a free place to live while draining the hot water tank.

Well, not anymore, Evie thought, daring to glance in Liam's vicinity, where Bev was now red in the face, still talking to him. The paper may not be working out as she had hoped, but tonight she was one step closer to becoming the well-rounded applicant the hospital in Boston wanted on their staff.

Sarah grimaced. "Onward. I need something…stimulating this time."

"As in, something that involves working side by side with an attractive man between the ages of twenty-eight and thirty-two?"

Sarah laughed. "That obvious?"

"Only a little," Evie said, thinking of her comments about Liam. Sarah was boy crazy, and clearly her dreams of starting over in a new town hadn't turned out as she had hoped. Evie felt like suggesting that she explore a town a little bigger if she needed more selection, but at the same time she hated to lose her friend. Here in Oyster Bay, friends became like family. You saw the same faces every day.

Like Liam's. There would be escaping him if she stayed, which was precisely why she couldn't.

"Here," she said, randomly stopping at a sign-up sheet for the pie baking contest. Last year, Abby's success had come as a surprise to the entire family other than Mimi, the Harper cousins' paternal grandmother, who taught Abby the recipe herself, and still felt she was somewhat entitled to the ribbon Abby now proudly displayed at the Harper House Inn, along with a front-page article on her food truck offerings at the Summer Fest.

"I don't think I can sign up for this one. I have to watch my figure in case Mr. Right shows up!"

"Did I hear someone say Mr. Wright?"

Oh, dear, now Bev was all wild eyes as she eagerly moved toward them, nearly pushing aside poor Linda McKinney in the process. Sometimes, Evie didn't know how Linda had the patience to be Bev's friend for so many years.

"You know my Timmy's destined to take over the pharmacy," she said bluntly to Sarah, who looked so panic stricken that Evie had to cram a cookie in her mouth to keep from laughing out loud. "A real businessman, my Timmy. And a true gentleman, as well. I raised him, I should know. He always holds a door open for a lady." She folded her hands and nodded once, as if that was that.

Evie saw the lump roll through Sarah's neck she gulped, clearly struggling to digest all this information that was coming at her at once.

"Thank you, Mrs. ..."

"Wright!" Bev barked, then patted her name tag proudly. "Mrs. Wright." She leaned in close to Sarah, giving her a little smile as she said, "Mother of Mr. Right." She backed up. Wink, wink. Sarah managed to titter in response before looking at Evie deploringly.

Catching Evie's eye, Bev suddenly straightened and cleared her throat. "There's nothing wrong with being proud of my son."

Evie lifted an eyebrow. Bev had no doubt read her response and knew where Evie stood on Bev's matchmaking. "I think it's wonderful that you love your son, Mrs. Wright. May we all be so lucky."

A pang in her chest caught her by surprise, but she tucked it quickly back into place, something she'd mastered over the years. When May rolled around and everyone in school was asked to make a Mother's Day card, she made a card for her father instead, or sometimes even Hannah. When other girls talked about back to school shopping with their mothers, Evie was happy to announce that she had an aunt who was taking them shopping...in Portland. And when other girls talked about prom dress shopping, Evie just gave a bored smile, because she had no interest in going to prom, not with finals right around the corner.

Now, looking back, she thought of all she'd missed. Yes, Bev might be overbearing, but no one could question her devotion to her son. Whereas Evie's mother hadn't given her a second thought ever since she'd left town when Evie was just a baby.

Perhaps Evie's statement triggered something in Bev, who had been their next-door neighbor since Chip first bought the house, before Hannah was born, because her expression softened for a moment before she patted Evie's hand. "You'll find love, dear. You just need to get that nose of yours out of those books for a minute!" She licked her bottom lip and leaned in close. "I'm sure there's an eligible man in town who would love to get you out of the house for a night!"

She waggled her eyebrow and grunted a few sounds, as if encouraging Evie to nod her head, consent to what was clearly an invitation on poor Tim's part.

Now it was Evie's turn to look at Sarah for help, but Sarah had fled, leaving her alone, no doubt desperate to get away before Bev cleverly set up a date for next Saturday night, no excuses accepted.

She opened her mouth to give a polite reason to part ways, but all that came out was a squeak when she saw Liam walking toward her, a slow grin on his mouth, his hands jammed in his pockets.

Never one to miss a hint of conflict or drama, Bev stood a little straighter and watched Liam approach with a look of interest that bordered on panic. "Ah, good. I was waiting to see if he'd come talk to you."

She gave a little wag of her finger as she walked away, back to Linda, who was quickly refilling her punch, making Evie wonder for a moment if it was spiked.

Evie was so confused by Bev's comment that she wondered for a moment if gossip had spread around town that she and Liam had a...thing...this summer that she almost stopped caring that Liam was now standing next to her, a mischievous gleam in his eyes. She blinked up at him, finding herself furious at how amusing he found all of this to be.

"You're in trouble," he said.

She stifled an eye roll and shifted the weight on her feet in impatience. So this is what Bev had meant: she wasn't pleased with Evie's response to her letter and had complained to the boss. Nice.

"Bev has been my next-door neighbor all my life. I'm used to dealing with her."

"That's not what I meant," he said with a lift of an eyebrow.

She frowned, studying his face for a hint of jest, but realizing with an uptick in her pulse that he wasn't joking with her at all. "What do you mean, trouble?"

She was going to be fired. He had decided that this arrangement was too awkward, that was it. But no, she could sue him for that, couldn't she? She had rights, after all. And besides, what had she done wrong?

She had arrived at work early, every morning this week. She'd replied to every single letter that hit her inbox, even to those that would never see print! She kept her desk clean, unlike Tony, who had left a rotting salami sandwich on a stack of old newspapers since Wednesday.

Still. Trouble and Evie Donovan didn't mix. Evie had never been issued a demerit. She was only ever called in to see the principal to learn that she was, again, student of the month. Still, she had walked that hallway to the front office as if she was walking the plank of a ship. She feared trouble. She hid from it. And now, yet again, she was facing it head on.

"What…what?" She couldn't even ask. She couldn't even speak. Her mind was racing and her face was starting to burn and she was feeling a little faint, quite honestly.

He picked up the sign-up sheet for the cake walk and let out a long sigh. "Whew. I thought you took the last spot and this was the only thing I wanted to sign up for."

She all but snatched the board from his hand. "I'll have you know that this is all I wanted to sign up for." It was this or manning the pony rides, and she really didn't think she could handle the manure. But cakes she could bake. And even better, she could get credit for volunteering from the comfort of her own kitchen.

"Well, there are two spots left," he pointed out, looking at her sidelong.

She pinched her lips. Was he testing her or challenging her? Either way, she'd be damned if she let him think he had any sort of effect on her.

"Good, then we won't have to fight over it," she said, quickly snatching a ball point pen from the table and scribbling her name. She'd always prided herself on her perfect penmanship, but today her hand was shaking and the second half of her last name was nothing but a squiggly line.

"So you don't care if I sign up too?" He was lifting an eyebrow, his face otherwise expressionless.

"Care?" She snorted. "Why should I care?"

He fought off a little grin. "Just checking." He reached out, and for a moment, Evie wasn't sure what he was going to do. Was he trying to hold her hand, reach out and connect, explain that he was sorry, that he was madly in love with her and hadn't stopped thinking of her?

Oh. He was reaching for the pen. Of course.

Evie crammed a cookie into her mouth before she said something she would come to regret, but the irony of the situation wasn't lost on her. There was a reason why she wasn't a joiner. Life was so much less complicated when you were home alone with a good book.

Chapter Eight

The air had a decided chill when Evie woke the next morning. She showered and dressed quickly, eager to start her day off. Technically, the newspaper was always open, and there was an edition going out first thing tomorrow, but so long as she had her column submitted by five today, she was set, and she planned to have it finished long before then.

Her sister was already in the kitchen, eating a banana in front of the kitchen sink and looking out onto the back lawn, when Evie walked in, smiling at the smell of freshly brewed coffee.

"You're up earlier than usual," she observed. Normally, Hannah had to set two alarms, and she often slept through both. When they were younger, Evie and Chip would take turns flicking the light in Hannah's bedroom and yanking open the blinds, just so she wouldn't miss the school bus.

"Dan and I are taking Lucy out on Joe's boat today. If we don't get rained out." She frowned as she craned her neck for a better look out the window, toward the sky.

Joe was another classmate of theirs, in Hannah's grade to be exact. Now he worked for Dan's contracting business by day and dated by night. According to local gossip, he was now dating Amanda Quinn, a pretty blonde who owned a spa on Main Street. People were already taking bets to see how long this one would last.

Hannah turned away from the window. "I've been meaning to ask you…"

Evie stifled a groan and turned toward the cabinet to reach for a mug, happy for the moment to have her back to her sister. She really, really didn't want to discuss Liam or the paper or the summer or any of that right now, not when she had such a great day planned specifically to avoid thinking about any of those things.

"Have you read Kelly's letter?"

Evie's pulse skipped a beat as she walked over to the coffee machine and lifted the pot. Steam rose as the liquid filled her mug, for the simple pleasure that always accompanied the first cup of the day was lost.

"I haven't," she replied honestly. She had no excuse for it, at least not one that Hannah would accept, not unless she wanted to dig up all the old wounds that had been a wedge in their relationship until recently.

"Oh." Hannah leaned back against the counter, seeming to absorb this information.

Evie sighed. "It's been a crazy week, starting a new job and…" No reason to touch upon the subject she wished to avoid. Besides, Liam being back wasn't a good enough excuse. In Hannah's eyes, family was family. They just had a slightly different definition when it came to the word.

Evie had gone her entire life without having a relationship with Kelly—or their mother. She didn't feel the rush now anymore than she did when Hannah announced she was moving to California right after graduating from high school. She'd balked at Hannah's offer to come visit her on the West Coast. As if! Evie was horrified at the idea of betraying Chip like that, and angry at Hannah for not factoring his feelings into her plans. But it wasn't so complicated for Hannah. Hannah loved her and loved Chip, and she saw no reason not to try to love their mother and their other sister too.

Evie opened her mouth to tell Hannah that she'd get to it, that she'd respond, maybe even today, but she wasn't sure that was true. She was happy with her world as it was. She hadn't felt the urge ten years ago and she didn't feel it now. And once she let Kelly in, she couldn't go back. The dynamic would be changed. Nothing would ever be the same again.

"She's just trying to connect with you," Hannah said, an edge to her tone that Evie didn't appreciate but one which shamed her all the same.

She nodded and went upstairs to grab a jacket. She'd reply to Kelly. She would. But not until she was ready.

*

Kelly couldn't believe it. She honestly could not even believe it. There it was, on the screen, black and white. A letter from her sister.

Well, not a letter per se, but a response, and better yet—advice!

Kelly skimmed the column so quickly that she barely absorbed a word, so great was her excitement that she and Evie had forged a connection, even if Evie wasn't aware that it was Kelly she was responding to, Kelly wouldn't let that burst her bubble. She took a few deep breaths and took the laptop over to her couch, where she leaned back against the stack of throw pillows and started over, properly, from the beginning. She could almost picture her sister reading the letter she had sent, considering Kelly's dilemma, giving thought how to respond. It was as if Evie were right here, in this very room, having listened to Kelly pour her heart out and now responding in the wise manner that was reserved for older siblings.

Kelly read the article, three times, because that was how many times it took her to get over the shock that at the very bottom, her sister had actually suggested that she knit.

Kelly loved to knit! Just Friday night that woman at the store had complimented her on the scarf she was wearing. She had an entire closet full of these scarves, things she'd made because it relaxed her…just as Evie said it would!

Did she know? Kelly tried to play back all her conversations with Hannah over the years and decided that really, Hannah wouldn't have bothered to mention any such thing. Hannah probably didn't knit, they had never knitted together, and besides, Kelly was always tinkering with crafts—there was the water color phase, the mosaic phase, where she'd turned a flea sale coffee table into a real piece of art, and of course the ill-fated ceramics phase, not her thing at all. She'd tried quilting, and she and Hannah had tried to make clothes one summer on an old Singer that Kelly had gotten for Christmas when she was fourteen. But knitting? Not Hannah's thing.

Knitting was Kelly's thing. A thing that she had forgotten she had loved, because she was so busy ogling over Brian and then, later, crying over him.

And now, from across the entire country, her sister she had never met was suggesting to her that she do something she actually loved.

Well, there was no other way to look at it. She would take Evie's advice. Today, in fact! She would shower and dress and go to the store. And she would knit.

They may not have met—yet—but for the first time Kelly was filled with a true hope. She picked up the phone and called Lindsay, impulsively inviting her to brunch at Jolene's, a place she used to go with her parents on special occasions and where she hadn't been in years. This day called for celebration!

It was cool outside, and so she dug out one of her fancier creations from her pile of knit wear—a soft, merino cowl in a lovely shade of grayish blue, and paired it with a black sweater and jeans. Her shoulders were squared, her chin was high, and by the time she pushed through the doors of Jolene's an hour later, she felt downright giddy.

Lindsay stared at her in disbelief. Her jaw was even a little slack. "Wow. You look great."

"Thank you! I feel great!" They followed the waitress to a table near the window which lent a view of Nob Hill. Another sign that today things were going to turn around for her. "I heard from my sister," she confessed in a low voice once the waitress had left.

"Hannah?"

"No," Kelly said, barely able to hide her smile. "My other sister."

Kelly was rewarded by Lindsay's eyes turning wide with surprise. "She replied to your letter?"

Oh. Kelly had forgotten about that part. Back when she was still at the commercial real estate firm, she and Lindsay would spend an hour at lunch catching up on their days. They knew the ins and outs of every transgression and drama, including that Kelly had finally worked up the courage to send Evie a letter in the box of items Hannah had left behind at the bedroom she'd used at Kelly's childhood home. Loraine had been going through everything one day when Kelly stopped by, something she rarely did now that she had her own apartment, but it was her father's birthday and they were having a cookout. Kelly had offered to send the box herself—most of her correspondence with Hannah was done over email or text or the occasional phone call, but the excuse to send an actual piece of mail? Well, that led to other possibilities, like reaching out to Evie, too, something she was too chicken to do over email. It was too instantaneous. There was too much room for immediate rejection.

"She wrote to me," was all Kelly could say, even though she felt her spirits sinking. Yes, Evie had responded to her, and it was a glorious, wonderful, elating feeling. But she had responded to someone who had written to her article. She was being professional. She wasn't being a sister.

"What did she say?" Lindsay overturned her mug so the waitress could fill it with coffee.

"She told me that I should go back to the gym, and that the only person who should be afraid to show their face there is Brian. And Shannon." Evie turned her own mug over and watched the waitress fill it.

"Wow! You've already told her about Brian?"

"Yes," Kelly replied honestly, because, well, she had.

"Wow!" Lindsay said again, shaking her head. "And here I thought you'd be all upset today about what happened at work and I'd have to cheer you up."

"Ugh," Kelly replied, happy to be on a new topic. "I don't really miss that place at all. It wasn't a good fit for me."

"They moved Romy into your cube. She clips her nails at her desk. I wish Darren would give you your job back," Lindsay said miserably.

Kelly couldn't help but laugh. "Well, I'm sorry for your situation but I don't think Darren will take me back. I am surprised he let me go, though. Is being late for work a few times really such a big deal?"

The silence on the other end of the table was her answer. Well, she thought as she reached for her menu and skimmed it, lesson learned. She wasn't going to let it ruin her day. Today would be a turning point. Today she was determined to cling to the good feeling she had when she woke up this morning.

Suddenly, Lindsay was hissing her name. Not whispering, hissing. Urgently. Alarmed, Kelly set down her menu and stared at her friend, seeing the fear that filled her eyes where just a moment ago surprise had been.

Oh, no. No. It couldn't be. Was Brian here? Shannon? Both of them? Brian knew that she used to come here as a kid with her parents! Surely he wouldn't steal this from her too? But then she thought of what her sister had said, that she should stake her claim, and she set her jaw as anger set in. So help her, she would order the stuffed brioche French toast with a side of seasoned potatoes and she would enjoy every bite of it. It would take a hell of a lot more than Shannon and Brian to ruin this day for her.

"Is it Brian?" she whispered back, her chest beginning to pound.

Lindsay shook her head, and Kelly couldn't help but breathe a sigh of relief. "It's…"

"Darren?" Kelly asked, and then, with dread: "Betsy?"

"No," Lindsay said, looking now like she was torn, as if she might even cry. "It's…it's your mother, Kelly." Her voice was gentle, filled with regret, even, and Kelly looked at her quizzically. She may not have the best relationship with her mother, but it wouldn't be exactly terrible to run into her.

She turned her head around at the same time that Lindsay said, "Wait!" but she hadn't waited, and it was too late now. There, at the far end of the room, was her mother, all right. Kelly would recognize that thick brown ponytail anywhere, and the oversized sunglasses she always wore, even indoors and even on cloudy days. She was laughing, leaning in against the tabletop, being spoon fed the rice pudding that the place was known for and that she always ordered, every time they came here, even though Kelly's father said it was old-fashioned.

But she wasn't with Kelly's father. She was with another man, a man with a lean body and a man bun. A man who was now wiping the corner of Loraine's mouth with the pad of his thumb and leaning in for a—

Kelly whipped around. Lindsay looked like she actually

was crying now. "I'm sorry, Kelly."

Her mind was spinning and she was trying to place the guy, because she knew him from somewhere, she was sure of it. It wasn't every day you saw a man bun, after all. She turned around for a second look, and it all fell into place. Of course. Loraine was with her yoga instructor. Chaz. Could it get any more cliché than that?

Her first instinct was to call Hannah. Really, who else was there that would care that her mother was doing the nasty with Chaz, a man who lit incense and wore spandex. But then she remembered that their mother's infidelity was a sore spot for Hannah; after all, it was pretty obvious she'd been two-timing Chip.

She couldn't call her father. What would she say? Better yet: what should she say? Should she say something or nothing? Would he be hurt or would he be angry? Both, if he felt anything like she did. The thought of it tore her up.

Dr. Chandler would know what to do, but he was still in Europe.

"Don't be sorry," she told Lindsay, when she could finally speak. "It's not your fault."

It wasn't anyone's fault but Loraine's. It was no mystery that her own existence hadn't been planned. Loraine had grown bored of her life with Chip, depressed by life in a small town, tied down to a man who worked nonstop at a restaurant and two young daughters, who seemed like her sole responsibility half the time. When a chance to break free of domestic responsibilities presented itself, she jumped. Oh, to hear her spin it, she couldn't help herself. Kelly's father, like so many people, it seemed, was vacationing in Oyster Bay one summer, and Loraine fell madly in love. She thought he was offering her a life that was different than the one she'd grown to resent. A life in a big, exciting city. A life that was carefree and not challenged by warming bottles and changing diapers, and watching daytime talk shows, or going to the park. And then Kelly came along. Kelly's father had been thrilled, and what could Loraine do but hope that this time she'd feel differently. And she had, she'd grown, she'd claimed she'd changed. She felt bad for what she'd done to Hannah and Evie, and even Chip. She was young, and not ready for that kind of life yet.

But did she feel bad for what she'd done to Kelly's father? Did she feel bad for this?

"We should probably go," Kelly said hurriedly. "I don't want them to see me."

"Are you going to tell her that you saw her?" Lindsay asked, as they discreetly slid a few dollars onto the table and pushed back their chairs.

"I don't know what I'm going to do," Kelly admitted as they hurried from the restaurant. But she had a feeling that she knew someone who would know just what to do.

She'd email Evie.

*

It had started to rain shortly after Evie walked into

Books by the Bay, and the temperature was dropping without the warmth of the sun. From the looks of it, it wasn't going to let up anytime soon.

Evie was grateful for the overcast conditions in a way; it gave her an excuse to skim the shelves, maybe even settle into one of the big, oversized armchairs that were spread through the shop and read for a bit. If it were still sunny and warm she would have gone to the beach. But lately, going to the beach felt wrong. It drummed up memories that now felt like a sham.

Trish McDowell was sitting on a stool behind the register, her reading glasses sliding down her nose as she frowned at a stack of paperwork. She was a dedicated shop owner, always matching or exceeding the seasonal decorations that the other storefronts boasted, and behind her Evie could make out some cornstalks, pumpkins, and colored leaves, which would no doubt be put out on October first, first thing.

October first was tomorrow, Evie realized with a jolt. And that meant that next weekend was Fall Fest. And another opportunity for her to be stuck with Liam.

Evie sighed and picked a book on managing grief off the new releases table.

"Evie," Trish suddenly said, and Evie looked up to see Trish looking at her with interest. "You might be able to help me."

Evie set the book down, feeling her spirits lift all at once, and not just from the distraction from feeling sorry for herself. Helping people was her specialty. This was what she had set out to do.

"You work for the paper now, right?" Trish slid her glasses off her face and set them on the stack of papers on the desk.

Evie grinned. "Ask Evie at your service!" She couldn't deny the thrill when anyone asked her advice or shared a problem. Trish, however, seemed to have other ideas.

"That publishing guy from New York took over, right?"

Evie froze in place at the front table. "Er…yes."

"Think he knows any authors who might live in driving distance of here and want to do a reading to promote their book?" Trish asked hopefully. "Jack's been great—I mean, J.R. Anderson," Trish laughed, referring to his famous pen name. "But we need more events to stir up interest and keep things from getting stale. I thought this publishing guy might know someone."

"I suppose he does, but I'm not sure I could help. We're not close," Evie replied, hating that shouldn't help Trish nearly as much as she hated to think that she and Liam meant nothing to each other. They'd only spent two weeks together, sure, but a lot could happen in two weeks, and, well, it had felt real. Better than real. It had felt right.

"Oh, well," Trish said airily. "Worth a try." She smiled as Kat, her part-time assistant, took over the register. "The boys are supposed to have a baseball game today," she said, glancing worriedly to the front of the store where rain spattered against the bay window. "Here's hoping it blows over soon."

"See you," Evie said, as Trish took her coat from the rack. She turned back to the shelves, feeling anything but relaxed. Jesus! Everywhere she went, it was Liam, Liam—

Liam.

She swallowed hard and stared at the man who was grinning back at her, his hair slick with rain, the shoulders of his camel colored sweater damp. She looked around for Trish, eager to pass him off, but Kat was now restocking some paperbacks and the back door slammed shut before the store fell otherwise silent. Normally, Trish had some background music going at least. But no such luck today.

"Hello," he said. His eyes were unwavering, as if he was searching for something from her, waiting for more than just common pleasantries.

"Hello," she said, trying to turn back to the shelf, but not able to because Kat was behind her now, grunting something about how no one alphabetizes anymore and do they know how much more work this has created for her? With a heaving sigh, Evie heard her drop a stack of books to the table beside her, muttering that now she would have to shelve everything properly.

Evie caught the lift of Liam's brows and felt herself smile. But no, no, she wouldn't give in. It was too easy to give in. The man was charismatic. He was a cool New Yorker, just like Sarah had said.

She took another step backward, and all but collided with Kat, who gave her a stern look and pushed her glasses higher on her nose.

Well, how was this for awkward? She was sandwiched between a disgruntled employee and the one man she desperately wanted some distance from. She'd planned to make a day of this, and now she would have to leave before she'd even scanned the back copy of a single book. And it was raining. And she hadn't thought to bring an umbrella. And that wasn't like her. Normally, she was overly prepared for everything.

What was happening to her?

She looked up at the man who seemed to find all of this perfectly amusing. This was what was happening to her. Him. He had come into town, shaken up her life, and made it suddenly so much more exciting. And then he had come back again and made her remember that all those blissful summer nights were part of another world, as if they had belonged to another person and not her, and that, even if she wanted to, she couldn't ever be that person.

She eyed the door, looked out on the rain-soaked potted yellow mums that were in full bloom, and the puddles that seemed to grow with each passing second. She thought back on the advice she had just given a poor girl who was avoiding her ex. (Who could it be, she'd wondered. It didn't match anyone in town that she knew of, unless someone had managed to keep their personal drama more private than was typically permitted in

Oyster Bay.)

She would stay, she decided. After all, she was here first. But to her dismay (and maybe, a twinge of displaced hope), Liam showed no signs of leaving.

"Looks like we're stuck here until the rain lets up," he said.

"I was just going to sit down and work on my article," Evie said, even though she hadn't planned on any such thing. She'd brought her laptop so that she could stop by Angie's later, have a coffee and polish a few things before sending it off. But now, it seemed like the perfect excuse. She was busy. He should leave her alone. Message sent.

Kat had wandered into the children's section, releasing audible sighs of frustration, and Evie hurried to the nearest armchair, a sense of victory filling her when she sank into the seat. She had barely retrieved her laptop from her bag, opened it, and pulled up her article, when she sensed a male figure dropping into the chair beside her, heaving a sigh as he did so.

She shot him a sidelong glance, her mouth pinched in concentration and disapproval. There were many other chairs in this store.

"You know, I enjoy reading your articles," Liam said, surprising her.

She blinked, not sure what to say to that. She'd never been good at taking compliments. They made her nervous, and she tended to laugh or apologize. But right now Liam was her boss, and so she simply said, "Thank you."

"What made you want to be a therapist?" he asked, and Evie was now forced to look at him properly. He was leaning back in the chair, one leg hooked on the other knee, looking at her with interest.

"I don't know," she said, wondering how much she should share. She didn't want to let him in, tell him anything more than he already knew. He knew the basics, of course. Her sister. Her father. Cousins. She hadn't mentioned Kelly or her mother, only that she didn't see her mother much. He knew about The Lantern and he knew about her time growing up in Oyster Bay. But other than that, they didn't share. They didn't need to. There were other things that they'd talked about and laughed about. They hadn't needed to go deep to find that connection—something that had shocked her. It was the ease of his company, she supposed, the way he thought to bring her the chocolate-covered blueberries, and the little smiles he would give when she thought he wasn't looking at her. The way he'd kissed her good-bye.

"My sister is older than me but a lot of the time I felt like I was the one looking out for her. And my dad was a single parent. He had a lot going on. I wanted to help, and when I helped, I liked to see how it made him feel. He seemed happy, relieved, and well, his life seemed better. I guess I liked the way that felt and I wanted to keep doing it."

Wow, she hadn't meant to say so much, but it was the truth, wasn't it?

"Is that why you helped at the restaurant over the summer?"

"Something like that," Evie said, stiffening. No need to tell her boss about her inability to land her dream job in Boston. She needed to keep the job she had, at least until she found something else. "Why'd you take the job at the paper?" she asked, genuinely curious but also eager to take the attention off of herself.

He chewed his lip, his eyes a bit hooded as he shifted them to the window. "Guess I needed a change."

People usually didn't make changes without a reason, and leaving New York City for a small town in Maine didn't seem like something anyone would do without just cause. She waited, to see if he would elaborate, but all he said was, "What's your next topic?"

Right. Back to work. She tried to push aside her disappointment, but she couldn't help it, it was there. Chatting with him, however briefly, had reminded her of how it felt to talk to him, sit with him, be with him.

"I'm responding to a man who is struggling to move on with a relationship," she said matter-of-factly.

Liam looked at her warily. "Not this Don guy again?"

Evie laughed. Don's letter had finally made yesterday's edition, and only because he had talked about his problem in broader strokes. "No, not Don. Although he does write every day."

"Every day?" Liam looked appropriately horrified, but Evie just laughed.

"He's harmless, and I'd like to think I'm helping him."

"But you don't publish his letters every day," Liam pointed out.

"No, but I do reply to them." Evie tapped on her keyboard to pull up her email account but stopped when she sensed that Liam was staring at her.

"You reply to all his letters?"

"I reply to all the letters I receive," Evie said. "People are asking for my help. Just because they don't make the paper doesn't mean that they shouldn't get a response."

Liam stared at her for what felt like far too long of a time, making her shift in her seat. Finally, because she couldn't stand the strange expression on his face anymore, she said, "This is a man who lost his wife. He's been unable to move forward since her death."

Liam's jaw twitched. After a moment, he said, "Sounds like a difficult topic."

"It is," Evie agreed. "On the one hand he feels faithful to his wife and doesn't want to betray her. On the other hand, his wife is gone and he is still living, but in many ways, he isn't allowing himself to live at all."

Liam nodded thoughtfully. "Do you have any experience with this type of thing?"

"Not first hand, no." Evie shook her head. "But…I know how it feels to be torn between two sides. To want something that makes you feel guilty. And…to not have a member of your family with you like they should be."

She thought of Hannah, and how she'd left them behind to go to California, how all she'd wanted to do was connect with family but had instead felt guilty as a result. Or maybe, made to feel guilty. And then, because she couldn't help it, she thought of her mother. It was a loss, she knew it was, but it had never hit her the way it hurt Hannah. She'd never allowed it to.

"I think the important thing is to think about the source of the guilt. Why does he feel so guilty for moving on with his life?" Yes, she'd start with that. It was entirely possible that the person would reach out to her again. She hoped very much that he would. He was lost, in pain, and he was living in limbo. She wouldn't wish that on anyone.

"You're very insightful," Liam said, and there was a flicker of surprise in his face now.

Evie smiled. "I just try to help."

He seemed to want to say something for a moment but then thought better of it. "Well, I look forward to reading your article," he said, motioning to the window. "Looks like it's slowing down out there. Think I'll make a getaway while I can."

She nodded. She should be relieved to see him go, to know that she could now go about her day the way she had intended, but once again, Liam had strolled in and messed with those plans.

"I'll see you at work tomorrow?" He phrased it like a question, as if he wasn't so sure she would show up, and for a moment, she felt guilty, thinking of the resumes she'd sent out, and then wondered if she'd hear back from any of them.

"See you tomorrow," she said, and watched as he went, wishing that her heart didn't feel like it was pulling in three different directions as he opened the door and stepped outside.

Wishing for a lot of things, she realized. And what good ever came from that?

No use thinking of her own problems, she decided. She turned back to her laptop. Time to help the widower.

Chapter Nine

Back when he was in New York, Liam used to measure his days by the way they were now versus the way they used to be. There was the restaurant on the corner of Fifty-Seventh that he and Ellen used to go to on Sunday afternoons in the fall. There was the park bench that they sat on one time and ate bagels, straight from the bag. But here in Oyster Bay, every aspect of his routine was new, from the place where he grabbed coffee and a sandwich for lunch (Angie's) to the place he had a beer after work (Dunley's). He knew it was owned by Ryan Dunley, Bridget's first husband and her daughter Emma's father, but Jack seemed cool with it, and besides, it seemed you couldn't go anywhere in this town without running into a conflict of interest, and so, in an effort to avoid The

Lantern upon his return, he'd chosen Dunley's. The burgers weren't so bad, either.

Now, though, there seemed to be little point in staying away from The Lantern. Tonight he was craving a lobster roll, and not the kind they sold at the Clam Shack, the beachside joint with the picnic tables and weather-worn dock. He'd eaten at The Lantern twice on his summer visit, and it was clear that Chip Donovan knew his way around a kitchen.

Liam looked up from his computer screen. Tomorrow's edition had been put to bed—the usual stories about the Main Street renovation, the progress of the dock expansion, even an entire article devoted to the upcoming Fall Fest. It wasn't exactly hard news, and strangely, this didn't bother him. He was happy not to open the paper and read about crime and murder, terror plots and corruption. Still, he knew himself enough to know that eventually he'd grow bored, and so would the readership, if they hadn't already. Jim Stafford ran a well-oiled machine, but change was necessary. They'd never grow if they only focused on happenings around town.

Now it was already almost eight, and the thought of going back to the empty apartment filled him with dread. The Lantern was in the opposite direction of home, if he could call the space that, but he had time. *Time.* It was something he'd thought about a lot over the years. Why was it that some people were granted so much of it and others so little?

He'd asked Evie that, in the letter he'd submitted to her column on Saturday. The response had gone out in this morning's edition. "Time is what you choose to make of it," she'd said. How would Ellen have wanted him to spend it?

Not like this, at least, that's what everyone had told him. Ellen would want him to be happy, to laugh, love and be loved. Ellen would want him to think of the future, not the past. But she didn't know, couldn't know, just how impossible that was.

He locked up the office behind him and hurried down the street to the restaurant. It was crowded, especially for a Monday night, and Liam questioned the reason for a moment until he saw her, standing behind the bar. Her blonde hair was pulled back off her face and her back was to him as she filled a glass from the beer tap. She turned and slid it across the bar to a man who accepted it with a smile, and she grinned ruefully, shaking her head at him, and turned to take the next order, her smile slipping when she met Liam's eye.

"I thought you quit this place," Liam said.

She seemed flustered as her cheeks flushed, but she eventually jutted her chin. "I'm helping out my dad. It's a family place, after all."

Liam held up a hand. "How you spend your free time isn't any of my concern." He'd meant that she didn't have to worry, that as her boss it didn't matter, but instead it came out dismissive and harsh. The pinch of her mouth confirmed that he had misspoke.

"My shift just ended, actually," she said, and began fumbling with her apron strings behind her back. A groan went up from several of the men sitting at the bar, guys with beer guts and grease-stained shirts and leathery skin, who looked like they just got off a hard day's work. They were older, several wore wedding rings, and even though Liam knew that given the age discrepancy their interest in Evie was probably more a fondness than an attraction, he felt something in him stir. Jealousy? Maybe. Or maybe it was confirmation. People enjoyed Evie's company. *He* enjoyed Evie's company.

"Have you eaten?" He was just being friendly, he told himself, making up for looking like he didn't care, when in fact he did care. More than he wanted to. Suddenly the thought of sitting at the bar with a lobster roll and a beer made him feel lonely, more lonely than the thought of going home and turning on the television. And with Evie…well, he wasn't lonely at all. That was what had made her so different than the others.

When she didn't reply, he said, "You can tell me the best thing to order. My treat." He gestured to the dining room tables, most of which were open.

Evie shifted the weight on her feet, the bar still creating a boundary between them. "I should probably get home."

"I'd hoped to talk about the paper," he said. The fact that this could be done tomorrow during business hours was a fact he chose to ignore. The truth was that he wasn't willing to let her go just yet, even though that's what he should do. She was trying to walk away, doing what was best for both of them. Creating distance. What he'd tried to do. Planned to do. But was it what he wanted to do?

"Well, I *am* hungry," she finally said, giving him a small smile.

"Great," he said, sliding off his bar stool. She set her apron on the counter and stepped out from the behind the bar, and for one, horrible moment, he had the same feeling he did that first day when he came back to town, when he realized how much he liked her, and how much potential was there if he'd just let himself fall, and how much worse his life felt when she wasn't around.

He couldn't win, not in this situation. But tonight, he didn't want to worry about tomorrow. There was no promise of it, anyway. Tonight, he just wanted to live in the moment.

*

This wasn't a date. Evie told herself this over and over until she was forced to believe it, until she remembered how badly it had stung when Liam had told her, clear as crystal, that he wasn't interested in having a relationship with her.

Still, it felt like a date, especially when Liam ordered a bottle of the best Cabernet that Chip stocked.

"I know you don't drink much," he said as he filled her glass.

"But do you know that the first night you met me and helped me over to a chair, I was actually limping because of how bad the blisters on my feet were and not because I'd been over served?"

He laughed and stared at her in wonder. "You never corrected me."

She shrugged. "I didn't see a reason to. Sometimes it's easier not to explain things."

"Like the fact that you are actually a licensed therapist and not a bartender," he said flatly.

She gave a small smile and reached for her wine. "I guess I didn't feel like drudging up my past."

He grew pensive for a moment. "I can accept that."

"I wasn't myself this summer. I was lost, I suppose you could say. I had expected to get this one job in Boston, and well, it didn't work out."

"Lucky for me that it didn't," he said, lifting an eyebrow.

She stared at him, wondering if she should point out that just last week he had made it clear that what had happened between them was over. Was he trying to be kind? Let her down gently?

She decided to get back to the entire reason she had agreed to have dinner with him at all. "So, you said that you wanted to talk about work?"

"Did I?" Liam looked surprised. "It can wait."

This wasn't a date, this wasn't a date, this wasn't a date. "Nothing wrong, I hope?"

He shook his head. "Definitely not. On the contrary, your column is getting the most web hits of every page on our site."

"Really?" Evie beamed. She hadn't been expecting that. "I can't believe that everyone likes it." Her stomach felt funny as she reached for her wine glass. People were enjoying the column. They were writing her letters, she was receiving more each day. Some people, like Ron, and Bev, and poor Wally Jennings's daughter, wrote multiple times. She was helping people. She was connecting.

And she was going to leave it all behind first chance she got.

"I can believe it," Liam said. "You have a real way with people. It's why I liked you so much."

Her heart skipped a beat, but she pushed any hope she had back into place. This. This right here was why she had to move on with her life, start over again. She still liked him. Still wanted him to like her. And comments like this did little to help her. They just messed with her head and her heart all over again.

"And here I thought it was because I mixed a mean martini," she replied coolly.

She was flirting, damn it. She reached for her wine glass again, even though she should really keep a cool head. This wasn't like her, but then, with Liam, nothing was like her. She'd fallen for him, lost all reasoning and common sense. And she strictly advised her patients never to do this!

"Although there was the one complaint."

And just like that, Evie was back to reality, back to that horrible day when she'd received the phone call from the hospital in Boston, regretfully informing her that after very careful consideration, they had chosen another applicant. "Why?" she had asked, even though she knew she shouldn't have. She should have gracefully muttered her thanks, hung up, and had a good cry. But Evie didn't cry. Crying didn't change anything. But information did.

"Who?" she asked now, running through every person in town who could take issue with anything she'd said.

Liam lifted an eyebrow. "Beverly Wright really let me have it at that planning committee, as you know. Something about her son and how she won't be told to distance herself from his affairs, that she knows what's best? I was so caught off guard all I could do was nod my head for fifteen minutes." He was laughing now, and Evie was too.

"What can I say? Sometimes the truth hurts." She shook her head, thinking back to what Hannah had said about the advice she'd given Ron. "My sister says I'm too harsh at times."

Liam tipped his head. "Maybe that's why your column is so successful. Maybe people are afraid to hear the truth but need it just the same."

She nodded eagerly. He understood. But then, of course he did. That's what she'd liked so much about him. She didn't have to explain herself to Liam. She could just…be with him.

"Well, I hope it helps them," she said.

"I am positive that it does," he said, his tone so insistent, his eyes so sincere, that she allowed herself to lock hold of them for longer than she should have, long enough to feel something in her chest swell.

Their food arrived just then. Right in time, she thought, pulling herself together. She ate, quickly, even though she had no appetite anymore, and kept the topic firmly on the paper, on her readers, on their letters, and on their fellow coworkers' strange habits, like the fact that Tony disappeared at three o'clock every day for exactly fifteen minutes, and no one knew where he went.

"He calls his mother," Evie explained.

Liam couldn't have looked more shocked. "Here I thought he was taking a cigarette break."

"Maybe that too, but his mother has a hold on him firmer than Bev Wright has on Tim," Evie said, and they both laughed. "Don't let Tony's hard shell fool you. He's a bleeding heart under that black leather jacket."

"I guess we all have our walls up to a degree," Liam said, and for a moment, she assumed he was referring to her less than forthcoming two weeks with him this summer, until she saw the sadness in his eyes.

Interesting, she thought.

"This was nice," she said as they stood. Liam had insisted on paying the bill and she'd let him. Not a date, just a...work thing.

He was looking at her strangely as they pushed out the front door and stepped outside, as if he wanted to say something and wasn't sure he should, or as if he wanted to do something and wasn't sure he should. She waited, heart beating, to see what choice he would make. The temperature had dropped even more, and in the distance behind her, she could hear the waves lapping at the rocky shore.

He stepped back, giving her a bit of a sad smile. "It was nice. I'll see you in the morning."

"See you," she said, and tried her best to fight the flutter in her heart that was mixed with disappointment.

Liam was a nice guy. A smart guy. An incredibly handsome guy. And he was her boss. And that in and of itself should make all of this much more clear than it felt.

Chapter Ten

By the next morning, Evie had fifteen letters in her inbox, some from identifiable members of the community (oh, Ron) and others that remained a mystery, like the woman who had just discovered that her mother was being unfaithful to her father.

Evie leaned back in her chair and pondered that one for a moment, deciding that she would save that response until later, when she'd had time to think about it. It was of a personal nature, not something that was a good universal topic and therefore not a fit for her column, but one she would respond to, personally.

She started with the easiest, once again urging Ron to stay away from Dave's house and reminding him that no, showing up at Jill's place of business with a bouquet of flowers would not win her back. She'd told him the same thing at the bar last night, while she filled his beer and ordered him a burger, on the house.

Last night had been nice, she thought. And not just because she'd missed the camaraderie of the clientele at The Lantern. It had been nice talking with Liam, too. Almost like old times.

Before she had a chance to indulge in that thought, an email popped up on her screen. Subject line: A word? Sender: Liam.

With a thumping heart, she clicked on the email. Nothing was written inside. Was she expected to respond? Something told her that this was an invitation to stop by his office.

She stood, rousing a suspicious glance from Hannah, who was editing photos for tomorrow's edition. Last week the only time Evie left her chair was to hide in the bathroom during lunch, after all.

"Meeting with Liam," she explained, and Hannah's eyes rounded, just as Evie knew they would.

She wanted to tell her about last night, about the day before at the bookstore, too, but now wasn't the time, and besides, what was there to tell? That she and Liam had bumped into each other? That they'd communicated like civilized adults, maybe even been a little friendly? To say anything more would be tapping into hopes that had no reason to exist in the first place. Liam had let her know where they stood. He was her boss now. It was nothing more than that.

But it certainly felt like something more than that

when she knocked on his half-open door a moment later and poked her head around the corner.

His desk, she noticed, was strewn with papers, file folders, and pens of various colors. His coffee mug was a paper cup from Angie's, and there were two more in the recycling bin. "Walk with me for a refill?"

She narrowed her eyes. "There's coffee in the kitchen, you know."

He cringed. "Watery, I'm afraid. And I don't want to hurt Sarah's feelings."

Evie couldn't help but smile. He was a good guy. Caring and sweet really. For a moment she wished she still thought of him as a jerk. It was somehow easier that way, to accept that they couldn't go back to what they had over the summer.

"Coffee it is then," she said, waiting in the doorway as he stood, forgoing his jacket. Hers was back at her desk, and despite the drop in temperature, she didn't want to go back to for it. Hannah would already have a million questions when she returned, but at least then she could answer them frankly, whereas now, she really couldn't explain what was going on.

They walked through the lobby, past Sarah who was leafing through the bridal magazines she subscribed to, even though she hadn't been on a date in three months, as she liked to complain, and when Liam pushed the door open for her, Evie and Sarah exchanged a glance that said she had some explaining to do when she returned.

Angie's was just down the road, but Liam didn't seem to be in a rush. The wind was picking up, stirring up leaves that had already started to change their color, and Evie busied herself by looking in the shop window displays, each more elaborate than the next.

"I have a confession," Liam said as they reached the next corner.

Evie looked up at him, wondering where he was going with this. She was used to people opening up to her, admitting things they rarely told anyone else, but Liam was guarded, even a little aloof, with revealing personal details.

Perhaps that was part of his appeal, she figured. He was a mystery. A project. Someone she wanted to get to know better.

"I've been using work as an excuse to, well, talk to you."

Evie tried to fight the smile that was forming and failed miserably. "Oh. Well, you know that you can always talk to me."

"Can I?" He was looking at her, really looking at her, and for the second time in two days, Evie sensed that there was more that he wanted to say. "It's just that last week, I was surprised to see you, and I feel like we got off on the wrong foot."

Oh. That. She pulled in a sigh, suddenly wishing they were back at the office and that she was safe in her cubicle, answering readers' emails about their domestic disputes and problems with their bosses and romantic trials instead of dealing with the problems of her own.

"It's fine," she said, eager to shut down the conversation.

"No," he said firmly. "It's not fine. I feel bad, and I've wanted to apologize. It's complicated. My life…it's complicated."

"You don't owe me an explanation," she said, even though she wasn't exactly sure this was true. Sure, they hadn't made any promises, but she'd assumed things had ended because he lived in New York and she lived here. Now, she had the bad feeling that even if he wasn't her boss, he wouldn't be pursuing anything.

"I'm sorting through some things," he said, giving her a long look, as if that was all he could say and that he hoped it would be enough.

She looked at him, really looked at him, and she saw a sincerity there that hurt her almost as much as it softened her. "Well, as I said, if you ever want to talk, I'm here."

"Actually, there is one thing I want to talk about," he said, grinning. "I want to increase the exposure of your column."

"Really?" Her mind was racing. She wasn't even sure what to think about that. She had one foot out the door. Now she felt like she was being sucked back in. And not just back to the job, or to Oyster Bay, but to him. To those feelings.

"So maybe we can go inside for a coffee and talk about it? Or maybe, just talk?" His smile was shy, such a contrast to the tall, handsome, confident, and "cool" image he publicly portrayed, and Evie knew that for once, she couldn't talk herself into doing the rational thing.

"Why not?" she said, ignoring the nagging thought that there were many, many reasons not to follow Liam into that café, and the troublesome realization that she was behaving completely irrationally, and that it could only lead her off track...again.

*

Liam didn't know why he'd invited Evie for coffee any more than he understood why he'd written her that letter on Saturday, or why he had the strange desire to write her another one.

Maybe he needed help, like all the others who wrote in. Or maybe it was something more than that, something more specific. Maybe he wanted to test the waters, see how it felt to reveal the truth to her. He assumed he would feel guilty, just as he always did. Instead, he felt, well, better. A little better.

They each ordered a coffee—his black, hers with cream and sugar—and took a seat near the window.

"A lot of your readers seem to write in about relationship problems," he observed.

She gave a wry smile. "Well, I suppose it's the most common issue. Tensions at home. Unrequited love." Her cheeks flushed a little.

"You know what to tell them. You must have a lot of experience in that area." He watched her, carefully, wanting to know her past, the parts of herself she hadn't revealed on his visit in August.

"Oh, a boyfriend in Boston. Nothing too serious," she said, shrugging.

"I was married," he said, catching himself by surprise. It was more than he had admitted to her over the summer, more than he told most women, other than the ones who were already tipped off, who knew about Ellen, the accident.

But they didn't know everything. And those who did never understood.

"Oh." Evie frowned. "I didn't know."

"It's not something I like to share," he admitted.

"Did it end badly?"

"Does anything ever end well?" he asked.

She gave a wry smile. "True."

He knew this was the time he could open up, say more, tell her that he wasn't divorced, that no one had cheated, that actually he'd been very, very happy, so happy that it was hard to believe it had to end, and so abruptly. But it didn't feel right. That was his past and this was...Well.

He looked out onto the street, where hay bales were now grouped at the base of each lamppost, and signs for the Fall Fest were tacked to every tree. "So, I've been meaning to ask you..."

She was staring at him so intensely, her blue eyes bright and no longer hidden behind those severe glasses she wore to work on her first day. "Yes?"

He looked around the room, seeing if he recognized any one, before he leaned in across the table and said, "What exactly is a...cake walk?"

Evie sputtered into her mug and then burst out laughing. "You're kidding, right?"

Liam dropped back into his chair. "Actually, no. I have no idea what that is."

She squinted at him. "But you signed up for it."

He nodded. That he had.

"But why did you sign up for it if you didn't even know what it was?"she asked, looking at him strangely.

He stared at her, wondering if he should explain why, even if he couldn't explain it to himself. He wanted an excuse to be near her. Outside the office. To go back to that place in August when he felt, well, happy. Happy for the first time since Ellen died.

Even if he didn't deserve it.

But from the blush that was spreading up her cheeks, he figured he didn't have to explain anything.

"I assumed it was...easy."

"Easy?" She burst out laughing. "Because it's called a *cake walk*?"

"I went to be social, take part in the community. I didn't need a big challenge."

She sipped her coffee and took great interest in rearranging the sugar packets that were loose on the table. "A cake walk is a large stand of cakes, basically."

"And I volunteered to do what exactly?" he asked

slowly, eliciting another laugh from her. God, he loved the sound of it. It made him smile. It felt good to smile.

"You volunteered to help bake the cakes," she said matter-of-factly.

Whoa. Now selling a cake he could do, but baking? Their apartment in New York had a double burner. They used the oven for extra storage. They ate out or ordered in. He couldn't even say if the range in his new apartment was gas or electric. He had a microwave and a toaster oven and he didn't need anything else.

"I'm expected to bake a cake?" he repeated, the question coming out like more of a statement. He was going to bake a cake.

More like buy one.

"Not a cake. Cakes. Each person has to make three cakes, otherwise there won't be enough."

He stared at her and the glimmer in her eye. "Please tell me you're joking."

She sipped her coffee, doing a poor job of hiding her smile. "I'm not joking. You are expected to bake three cakes. By Saturday. I plan to start tonight. I can freeze the layers and frost them the morning of the festival."

"Frost them," he repeated, nodding, even as his mind was spinning. There would be frosting. And something told him the store-bought kind wasn't what they had in mind. "Is there a…bakery in town? Other than this place?"

Evie let her jaw drop. "A bakery? You can't *buy* your

cakes, Liam. You have to make them. Believe me, Dottie Joyce will know if any of those cakes was so much as made from a boxed mix, and she'll let everyone in town know it." She chewed her lip and blew out a breath. "Tell you what. We can do it together. My dad redid his kitchen over the summer and it has all the appliances we need."

He knew he should say no, get out before he got in, spare himself the guilt, the mixed feelings. But more than anything he wanted to spare himself the feelings he had all those long, lonely days in New York. The days he'd gotten away from.

"Does tomorrow night work?"

He mentally ran through his calendar, knowing that he was free. Other than Jack and Bridget, he knew no one here. He'd liked that idea. Now, he didn't. He felt better when he was with Evie. So much better than when he was without her. "Tomorrow night," he agreed.

Chapter Eleven

Kelly opened her computer first thing each morning, before she'd even had a cup of coffee yet, and went right to the *Oyster Bay Gazette*'s homepage, her breath bated, wondering if this would be the day she received a response from the latest letter she'd submitted to the Ask Evie column. As with yesterday and the day before, she let out a sigh of disappointment. Today's post was to a woman whose father was aging, who had locked himself out of the house three times last week, and who refused to give up the car keys, no matter how much the woman begged.

Kelly sighed and went to the coffee pot, filled it with water, and set it to brew. It was asking too much. She should be grateful that Evie had replied to her at all.

She added a splash of soy milk to her coffee when it

was finished and looked at the pile of yarn that was sitting on her coffee table. She had already gone through ten skeins since Sunday, and she had to admit, it had done wonders for her spirit. The more she knitted, the less she thought about Chaz and his man bun and the way he'd leaned across the table and spoon fed her mother.

Gah! She was going to scream. Right. She would finish her coffee while she job searched and then she would finish up the scarf she had started last night. She'd give them away as Christmas gifts, she decided. After all, people seemed to like them. Sure, she still wasn't back at the gym, but she was at least getting out, and the lady at the yarn store she'd discovered around the corner had said they even offered Tuesday night knitting sessions. Maybe she'd pop in next week.

She dropped onto the one bar stool she could fit in the apartment and logged into her email, wondering if anyone would have responded to the jobs she'd applied to yesterday (office assistant at a Pilates studio, marketing coordinator at a residential real estate firm, and research analyst at a law firm) and nearly jumped when she saw the email at the top of her screen. The sender was Evie. Evie Donovan, to be exact.

The day she had waited for had arrived!

Kelly was shaking so hard that she nearly spilled her coffee, but then slurped it instead, almost afraid to click on the email and see what was inside. Would Evie tell her to get lost, leave her alone, never send her another letter? Hannah must have provided Kelly's email address. It made sense. Who sent regular mail through the post anymore? Things could get lost. It took days. Of course Evie wouldn't have written back. Why hadn't Kelly considered this?

It wasn't until her coffee was finished and she had rinsed and dried the mug that she worked up the courage to open the email. She would face her fear. She would have her answer. And then…she would knit. Somehow having this plan in place made her feel better already.

She clicked on the link, her eyes processing a jumble of words on the screen before her mind could connect that Evie had actually written. That she hadn't said to buzz off.

Her heart was pounding out of her chest as she leaned in and scanned the words, barely registering them, but absorbing them all the same. She frowned. Wait. Evie was talking to her as if she knew her. She was talking about their mother! She was talking about an affair.

She was writing to her as Ask Evie.

And Kelly's email address didn't give any indication of her name. She was SunshineGirl93. A girl without a name. A girl who had submitted a letter. A girl who was now getting her response.

Without bothering to read the rest, Kelly closed her laptop. Her chest now felt heavy, and even though she'd just gotten out of bed, she felt exhausted. She looked at her knitting needles, at the beautiful pale grey angora she probably shouldn't have spent money on, and she walked past it, into the small bedroom that couldn't even fit a headboard or a dresser. She crawled back into her unmade bed and closed her eyes, but she couldn't sleep.

Somewhere on that computer was a letter from Evie. Not to her, not really, but still, it was something. Advice. A connection. An insight into the person she was. Maybe insight into why she was staying away, refusing to let Kelly into her life.

She stayed there for what felt like an hour but what was probably only ten minutes, and then she tossed off the duvet and walked back into the living area. Her laptop was still on the counter to her kitchenette. Her yarn was still on the coffee table.

She picked up the needles and purled a row. She did feel a little better.

She'd read Evie's letter, but later. After all, she had emailed. And something was better than nothing.

*

Liam arrived at seven o'clock, as planned, and even though they were going to be baking all night, something that Evie expected to be a messy endeavor, she'd worn her best cashmere sweater and jeans, telling herself that really, it was for herself more than the impression she was making.

Hannah was at Dan's house. She was spending more and more time there, which was fortunate, but still, Evie had double-checked her sister's plans for the evening, just in case. She didn't know what was happening between

Liam and her. Was he extending an olive branch, looking for a friend, or maybe, looking for something more?

Chip was at the restaurant, of course, and the ingredients were already out on the counter when the doorbell rang. Evie smoothed her ponytail and then her sweater, thinking she should have worn black instead of cream, but knowing it was too late now.

She opened the door, telling herself that really, the guy was just coming over because he was in over his head, even though she dared to hope that it was much more than that.

"I'm afraid I'm empty handed," he admitted in lieu of a hello. He pulled a bottle of wine from the grocery bag. "Except for this."

So it was going to be that kind of evening then. Something social. How social, she wasn't sure yet. Just like she wasn't sure just how close she should allow herself to get. Just last week Liam had said that the summer was an indiscretion. People didn't have sudden changes heart. She knew she didn't, much as she wished she did. It would be so much easier to not care at all for Liam, to not have this strange, fluttery feeling in her stomach when she caught his eye and he smiled.

"I have all the ingredients we need anyway," she said, leading him back to the kitchen, which Dan had installed over the summer. It was beautiful, with white glass front cabinets and a creamy, pale grey quartz counter. Her father had installed the highest end appliances, not much different than the ones he had in the kitchen at the restaurant. It was his dream kitchen, and one he had waited thirty years to have.

It saddened her just as much as it filled her heart with love when she thought of how long he had waited to treat himself. Her father was a businessman, but he was also, at heart, a chef. He'd built that restaurant with a dream, and worked night and day and holidays, too, just to keep it going. Every dime he made went back into the business or to his girls. He put them through college and he put Evie through grad school, and he never complained. Sure, there was the occasional cuss word when a cabinet knob fell off again or the oven took half an hour to preheat, but he never made them feel bad, never complained about shelving his wants and wishes for theirs. Over time, Evie realized that his wants and his wishes were for their happiness, not his. It was why she agreed to do things like attend school dances, so he wouldn't worry that she didn't fit in, and why she did the laundry, without asking. Why she wanted that big job at the hospital. Why she had stopped speaking to Hannah when she went to California, leaving them both behind...

When Evie graduated from her master's program last spring, Chip quietly decided to renovate the kitchen, never once mentioning the timing, or that he had put the plan on hold until his girls were settled. He was selfless that way, generous. He was everything to her. More than she would ever need.

How could she think about forging a relationship with

Kelly, without thinking of how it would make her father feel?

"This is a great kitchen," Liam remarked as Evie pulled a corkscrew from the drawer and handed it to him. He looked at her quizzically. "I assumed you would be the expert at this."

"My bartending days are over," she reminded him. No need to mention that she was on call to help out if anyone ever called in sick.

"Happy to hear it," he said, as he cut the foil from the bottle and screwed the cork off. "Though I doubt some of the regulars would say that."

"Oh, they still reach out to me," Evie laughed as she pulled two wine glasses from the cabinet and set them on the island. She gestured to the stack of recipes she'd printed out this morning before work. "I hope you're ready for a long night. Each cake has to be unique, you know."

"No, I didn't know." Liam filled their glasses and held his to hers.

"What are we toasting?" she asked, expecting something obvious, like a night of baking, or a first time for everything.

He surprised her by saying, "To fresh starts."

She clinked his glass, wondering what he meant by that, and telling herself that she couldn't read too much into it, no matter how badly she wanted to. He was new to town, new to volunteering, too, new to everything this town offered. Surely that was all it was. Even if it felt like a heck of a lot more.

They started with the most basic recipe: a simple yellow sponge cake with a chocolate butter cream. The mix came together quickly, and Evie was grateful for the task to keep her hands busy and her eyes focused on something other than the man standing across from her.

"Did your mother teach you do this?" Liam said as they slid the pans into the double ovens and Evie set the timer.

"My father," she corrected him, as she wiped her hands on a dishtowel.

He gave a small smile. "Of course. He's the chef, after all."

Evie rinsed out the mixing bowl and dried it slowly, wondering if she should bother elaborating but feeling like she could. He knew she didn't see her mother much. She had just never told him the extent of it. "My mother left us when I was just a baby. I never knew her."

Liam frowned. "I didn't know. I'm sorry."

Evie shrugged, giving the little smile she always gave when she had to offer up this explanation, like back in Boston, when people discussed holiday plans or asked who was attending graduation. She delivered the information casually, it was nothing new, after all, just a part of her that had always been there, but something inside her hurt just the same. No one in Oyster Bay talked about Loraine, not her father, not even Hannah. She wasn't a part of their lives and it was easier not to think of her ever being one, but she had been. Somewhere, far back in time, she had a mother. A mother who fed her and changed her and bought her clothes and toys. A mother who held her. It was hard to even think about. Impossible, really.

"My sister went to live out near her for about ten years," Evie said, as she began measuring out the flour for the dry ingredients. The next recipe was more adventurous: lemon. Chip's personal favorite, and hers too. "She went to college out west and then stayed with her after that for a bit."

"And you didn't visit?" Liam seemed perplexed by this, and Evie realized then how odd it must have sounded. Everyone in Oyster Bay knew about the infamous Loraine Donovan who had dumped two little girls on Chip and never returned, rumored to have left with a dashing tourist, confirmed when another child was born a short while later. They knew the story. They didn't need to ask. But Liam wasn't asking out of nosiness. He was asking because, well, maybe he wanted to get to know her. The real her. Not Evie, the breezy bartender who had casual summer romances and kept things light and fun.

"My sister and I have had some problems over the years," she started.

"Hannah? But you two seem close."

"We're fine now," Evie was quick to explain. She frowned suddenly. "At least, I hope we are. Hannah has a relationship with Kelly, my mother's other daughter, and she's hoping I will too."

"You have another sister that you don't know?" Liam seemed bewildered.

"It's not that I don't *want* to know her," Evie explained. It wasn't. It definitely wasn't that. She did want to know her, she just wasn't so sure how she felt about getting close to her. And how could you have a sister without being close? "I guess it feels strange. She knows my mother, and I don't. I'm happy with my life as it is, really."

"Are you?" he asked, and she nodded, but more and more she wasn't so sure of that. She'd thought she was fulfilled, content, that she had everything she could want and that nothing was missing. And then Liam came into her life, reminding her of how much more was out there.

Liam nodded thoughtfully. "Still. It's not easy to separate your emotions, is it? I mean, it's your mother."

"Do I sound cold to you?" she asked, wondering if she did, if this was her problem, if this was why it was so easy for her to block out the thought of Kelly's letter, sitting in a drawer upstairs, still sealed. "Like I don't care?"

He stared at her blankly for a moment. "Maybe it's not that you don't care. Maybe it's that you do. It's easier to shut off things that hurt you rather than face them."

She couldn't help but grin. "Well, look at you! Maybe you should take over my column!"

And maybe he would. If she got a job in Boston, she thought, feeling uneasy again. She hadn't heard back from anything yet, and maybe she wouldn't. She didn't know if that thought was depressing or a relief.

"I guess you could say that I speak from experience. I didn't move to Oyster Bay just for a career change," he said.

"I figured. Not many people move to Oyster Bay full time for career opportunities." She handed him the bowl of dry ingredients. "Sift," she instructed.

He frowned at the bowl of flour and baking powder, but did as he was told, hesitantly at first, until she nodded her approval. He stopped, looking up at her for a moment. "I told you that I was married before. But what I didn't tell you was that my wife…she died."

Evie blinked, trying to process this information and the image of him that had formed during the time they'd spent together. There hadn't been a hint of such a huge moment in his past, but now, looking back, something seemed to fall into place. "I'm sorry. I didn't know."

"It's not something I like to talk about. It's been two years. A lot of people in my life think that I should be over it by now."

"That's not something you can just get over," Evie said, thinking of the advice she'd given to the one person who had written in to her column about grief. Had she been too harsh? Too callous? Too unfeeling?

"I came to Oyster Bay hoping that I would escape the ghosts," Liam said, doing a terrible job of sifting those ingredients, Evie couldn't help but notice.

She took the bowl back, did it herself, or Dottie would never let her hear the end of how the lumpy batter had made for poor texture.

"In New York, everywhere I went, it was a memory of my past. Here, I have a chance of focusing on the present. At least that's what people tell me."

"Like Jack?" She smiled. Now it made sense. Jack had arranged the interview for Liam. He'd done it from a good place, because he had a big heart. He really was the perfect husband for her cousin Bridget.

"It was Jack's idea," Liam nodded. "He's been a good friend to me, and I know he wouldn't have suggested something that he didn't think would work out."

"And are you glad that you came?" Evie asked, setting down the sifter.

He was looking at her, so intensely that for a moment everything around them seemed to go still. "Very."

She blew out a breath, unaware that she'd been holding it in all this time and jumped when the oven timer went off. "I almost forgot about the cake."

He gave her a lopsided grin. "That makes two of us."

*

He hadn't expected to tell her about Ellen, but somehow it was easier, now that she knew, even if she didn't know that it was he who had written her the letter. They baked all six cakes in under two hours, thanks to the double ovens, and when they pulled the last one from the rack, Liam regretted that they were finished.

"That went by quickly," he said, draining what was left of the wine into both their glasses, even though he'd had two glasses to Evie's one.

"You enjoyed it then?" she asked as she set the pans to the side to cool. The other cakes were already wrapped in cellophane and set in Chip's industrial-sized freezer.

"I did actually. I never cook. Or bake. But it was engrossing. And fun," he admitted.

"Then you've found your flow," Evie said with a knowing smile.

"My flow?" He narrowed his gaze at her. "Don't tell me you're going to analyze me."

"Flow. It's basically something you do that is intrinsically enjoyable, something that consumes all your energy and pulls your thoughts away from everything else. I encourage all my patients—I mean, readers—to find their flow. Those that are good with their hands, or feeling anxious, I tell to knit. Those that are creative, I tell to paint. And you, well, you should bake. Who knew?" She gave him a little smirk and he picked up the nearest dishcloth and swatted her with it.

She laughed as her cheeks turned a bright pink. She was teasing him and he was enjoying it.

"So what's your flow?" he asked as he leaned back against the counter.

"Oh, I don't know that I have a flow, per se. I like to read. Sometimes it's nice to escape into a good book."

He cocked an eyebrow. "So you're hiding from your

issues by burying yourself into someone else's life?"

The space between her eyebrows crinkled. "I never thought of it like that. But maybe." She shrugged. "Sometimes it's easier to focus on other people. Not think about your troubles for a while."

He nodded. "That's why I volunteered for the Fall Fest. It got me out of the house."

"And into my kitchen," she said, giving him a long look. She wanted answers, answers he couldn't give. Promises he couldn't make. But a feeling, a feeling that he couldn't fight anymore.

He set his glass down, leaned in, and kissed her, hearing the gasp of surprise right before his mouth met hers. He kissed her, slowly, like they had all those nights on the beach, and she kissed him back, even though a part of him wasn't sure that she would.

"I like you, Evie," he said, when they pulled away. "I'm not used to liking people. It's new to me. It's why—"

She pressed a finger to his mouth and smiled. "I understand. You don't need to explain. We can take this slow. I'm in no rush."

He grinned, feeling better than he had in a long time. "Me either."

"We have all the time in the world," Evie said, and something in Liam's gut shifted. Time. There was that word again, that sense, that uncomfortable sensation that he associated with it.

He could fall down the dark hole again, ask himself

why he had time, or he could follow Evie's advice, and ask himself what he planned to do with it.

He leaned down and kissed her again.

Chapter Twelve

Liam was walking down Main Street the next morning, a bakery bag from Angie's containing a blueberry muffin in one hand, an extra-large paper cup of coffee in the other, when he spotted Evie, up ahead, waiting at the crosswalk. His pulse quickened in time with his feet, and he wove his way through the crowds that had already grown on the sidewalk despite the early hour—shop owners setting up potted mums, hay stacks, pumpkins, and gourds, and tourists in town for the upcoming Fall Fest weekend, recognizable by their slow pace, and their habit to stop at every window display and make a remark.

When he was closer, he held up a hand, tried to wave, but the bakery bag made it awkward and so he called out her name instead. "Evie! Hey, Evie!"

She seemed to frown and look from side to side before

she stepped out into the street. He was being impatient, probably. After all, in a few minutes he would see her at work. But he didn't want their first conversation of the day to be at the office. It would feel too complicated, and that was what he liked best about Evie. She wasn't complicated. She was straightforward. With Evie it was just simple, easy.

She was moving slowly, perhaps aware that she had heard her name, still on the lookout for who had called it out, so he tried again, a little louder this time as he grew nearer, managing to snag her attention this time. She stopped, turned, and spotting him, held up a hand, the smile on her face evident, even from a block away.

His heart sped up at the sight, but that brief moment of happiness was quickly replaced with something else, something all too familiar. Stone cold fear. A car. It was coming too fast, it wouldn't be able to stop at the intersection in time, if it planned to stop at all, and he wasn't sure it did. His mind seemed to process a hundred thoughts in a split second: he could run, or he could scream, or he could do both, but would it be enough? He estimated he had seconds, if that, and yet even though time was on overdrive, everything he saw and heard and felt in that moment felt like slow motion. He was back in the car with Ellen, it was raining, and they were lost, somewhere upstate that was so rural he had lost GPS tracking on his phone. There was a map, somewhere in the back, and Ellen said she would get it, but she couldn't reach, and he didn't pull over, didn't take the time to inconvenience himself because they wanted to get to the B&B before dinner, and it was he that had made that wrong turn about an hour back. So he reached back, fumbling, exasperated and cursing at this point and wishing they had stayed in the city. How many times had he wished they had just stayed in the city? If they'd stayed. If he'd booked some other trip. If he hadn't missed that turn. If he had just pulled over! By the time he saw the truck, it was too late. His mind knew it even as his arms jerked the steering wheel and his foot hit the brake. It happened so quickly it couldn't be stopped. But it happened so slowly that he could see the look of the driver's eyes right before they hit. The guy had a beard and brown hair and he was wearing a grey tee shirt. He heard the scream, the terrifying, horrible sound that would be the last sound Ellen ever made, and for a long time after, when he closed his eyes, that was all he heard. And then crying. And it took him a long time to realize it was him. "Ellen! Ellen!"

Evie. Evie! The screams were silent. In his head. Evie must have seen the panic in his face, must have followed his stare, because she turned, faced the car head on, and—

The world went still. Just a for a moment. And then it burst to life. People were running. The car was speeding off. He followed it, just for a moment, but this time he couldn't make out a driver. He snapped his head back, his stomach a wash of ice cold fear, and then he was running.

The bakery bag wasn't in his hand anymore, neither was the coffee cup. A crowd had already gathered around Evie by the time reached her, lying on the street, someone shouting to give the girl space.

The blood was rushing in his ears and his heart was beating so hard that he felt like he couldn't breathe. There was blood. God, there was blood.

"It's just a cut," he heard someone say. A sweet voice, a firm voice. It took him a moment to process that it was Evie's voice.

The relief did little to drown out the fear. It was still there. Stone cold. Paralyzing.

"What the hell was that guy doing?" someone else said.

"Did you recognize that car?"

"Did you see the plate?"

"Just the first three digits."

"Well, won't take Eddie Boyd long to figure it out," another said.

They were talking, everyone all at once, and somewhere in the distance was the wailing of an ambulance.

Evie rolled her eyes at him, but he saw the fear in them, the tightness of the brave smile. "I'm fine. I got out of the way." She started to stand, creating a murmur of concern from the crowd, and Liam reached forward, grabbing her just before she fell to the ground again.

"Sort of like the first time we met," she said, looking up at him.

Maybe it was, he thought. Back then he'd been the same man he was just now. Scared. Sad. Eager to hide from life rather than live it.

"Sit down," he ordered. "You might have a concussion."

He was scanning her, registering her injuries: two skinned knees, elbows too, a cut on her chin, and something with her ankle. God knew what else. There could be countless internal injuries. He didn't step back until the paramedics arrived, telling everyone to step to the side.

By now everyone in town had stopped what they were doing and were watching the scene. Evie's cheeks were red, and it was the first time he thought she might cry. "What is it?" he asked.

"It's all these people," she said, shaking her head.

"Everyone back up," said a male paramedic, someone that Evie was referring to as Mike, someone she'd probably grown up with, gone to school with. Maybe it was even an old boyfriend. Maybe it was a regular down at The Lantern.

"Everyone step back," a man that Liam recognized as Bridget's brother-in-law was saying now. He was wearing a uniform with a badge. He cursed as he crouched down to talk to Evie.

Liam backed up, wanting to give Evie space as much as he didn't want to leave her side, and looked over to see Hannah running toward them at full speed. The fear in her eyes no doubt matched his own. She was so out of breath, she was barely able to talk when she finally reached him. "Eddie called me." Spotting her sister, she cried, "Oh, God, Evie. Oh, God."

Evie looked sharply at her sister. "I'm fine, Hannah. Tell Dad I'm going to be fine!"

"Oh God! Thank God!" Hannah started to cry and Liam put an arm around her shoulder, until Chip Donovan did arrive, panting and out of breath, just as they were loading Evie into the back of an ambulance.

"They'll take her over to St. Francis." Eddie was speaking to Hannah and Chip.

"I'll drive," Chip said, and Hannah looked up at Liam, a question in her eyes.

"Take the day off," he said, without her having to ask. "Take as much time as you need."

"Are you coming?" she asked, and he hesitated.

"I'll follow," he said.

Hannah nodded, and ran off with her father without another word. The crowds had thinned now, the drama was over. People muttered their shock and concern as they strolled back to the sidewalks. Shopkeepers went back to their storefronts. Life resumed.

Up ahead Liam saw his bakery bag. The lid on his coffee cup had popped off when it hit the pavement. Now just a puddle of hot liquid was seeping into the cement. He walked back toward his apartment building. Down Main Street. All the way to the end. A left turn near Jojo's, then a right. His car was up ahead. He didn't know his way to the hospital, but he could look it up. GPS. He could go there, sit in the waiting room, wait for news, just like he had two years ago. By then the rain had subsided and the sky had opened up, bright and blue, almost turquoise. He remembered it because when he'd finally emerged from the building, from his fog, he'd stared at it for so long, weeping in despair, then screaming in anger. Why? Why?

He'd gone back into the waiting room, waiting for news that wouldn't come, but still he hoped against the hopelessness. He didn't drink the coffee they offered, or the celebrity magazines, or the crappy television shows that played with no volume in the corner, their subtitles streaming at the bottom of the screen. He didn't even know where he was, other than somewhere he wasn't supposed to be. It was supposed to be a weekend getaway. The start of something good.

He walked to the car now, opened the door, closed it again once he was inside. But he didn't start the engine. He'd promised himself then that he would never let himself feel this way again. The raw, cold grip of fear that made everything else disappear.

He'd promised himself. But it was just another promise he'd broken.

But he wouldn't break that promise again.

He didn't know how long he had been sitting in the car when his phone rang. It was a number he didn't recognize, and he stared at the screen for three rings before he answered.

"Liam? It's Hannah. Sarah gave me your cell number. Evie's fine. A few scrapes and a sprained ankle, but she was lucky."

Lucky. He was lucky. That's what they'd all told him. How lucky he was. His car had collided with a truck and he had walked away without an injury.

"She's asking for you," Hannah was saying, and Liam forced himself back to the present. To the future. Back from the past that seemed more real to him than ever before.

"Tell her I'm sorry," he said, clearing his throat. "Just tell her that. That I'm sorry."

"Liam?" Hannah sounded rightfully confused, and he knew he owed her an explanation, but it wasn't something he could explain, not even to himself.

*

Honestly! Evie didn't know what all the fuss about, even if she had to admit that she'd never been more scared, not even the time Hannah had dared her to climb the tree in the backyard to see who could go the highest and Evie, not being very experienced in risky endeavors but not one to turn away a challenge, had missed a branch and fallen, resulting in a broken arm and, happily, a month off the required morning swim lesson at camp. But this was even worse. One minute she was looking at Liam, remembering that kiss, remembering all those kisses and all those summer nights, her heart soaring when she saw that smile, that wave, and then, the next thing she knew there was a rush of speed, a car moving so quickly she wasn't sure how she would ever get out of the way in time. It was a black car, that was what she told Eddie. He sat beside her, his mouth a thin line of anger. Ah, Eddie. He'd been a teenager when he'd moved to Oyster Bay and she'd just been a kid. He was Margo's boyfriend back then. The kid with the rough past and a charitable uncle who had taken him in, trying to give him a second chance. And look at him now. On the force! Sheriff, to be exact. He was joining efforts with five neighboring counties to start a program for troubled teens. He wanted to give back, he'd said. He wanted to change people.

She'd always believed that people could change, if they wanted to. But a change of heart was something different. Maybe it could happen, she mused. Or maybe that was the pain killers talking.

"A black car? Not an SUV?"

Evie shook her head. "That's all I can remember other than the dive I took into the next lane." She gave him a wry smile, but he didn't seem to find this amusing.

"You could have been killed."

"But I wasn't," she said. Still, the thought unnerved her, how quickly life could change. If Liam hadn't been there, if she hadn't seen the panic in his face, hadn't been tipped off, would she still be here at all?

She shuddered at the thought. She couldn't think about that right now. But she did want to thank him.

Hannah poked her head back in the room and Eddie closed his notebook. "You know where to find me if you think of anything else. I can promise you we will find the bastard."

Evie smiled for real now. Eddie was a good guy. Margo was lucky to have him.

"Where's Dad?" Hannah asked as she slid into the chair that Eddie had just vacated.

"I sent him off to get me some pudding. You know Dad. He'd just sit and worry. He'll feel better if he can help in some way." Evie adjusted herself against the pillows. The nurse who had just left confirmed that she would be released in the morning. "Do me a favor and take him home tonight? No sense in all of us losing sleep tonight."

Hannah nodded, but there was a frown between her brow.

"You heard the nurse," Evie told her. "They're just keeping me for observation"

Hannah nodded again. "I know. We're all just worried."

"Well, consider me lucky," Evie told her, as she set her head back against the pillows. "If it hadn't been for Liam, I never would have turned around in time to see what was coming at me. Where is he, anyway?"

Hannah swallowed hard and looked down at her hands. "He's not coming."

"Oh." Evie pushed aside the disappointment. Last

night had been so wonderful, she'd gotten carried away. "Well, he has a paper to run and two of his staff are out…"

Hannah looked pained. "I don't think it's that. I talked to him. I told him you were asking for him. And he said to tell you that he was sorry."

"What do you mean?" Evie asked, but even as she spoke, she knew. Last night, just like those summer nights, was a fleeting moment. And this, right here, this was too real for Liam. Too serious.

"I'm sorry, Evie," Hannah said, shaking her head.

"Don't be sorry," Evie said, but her chest felt heavy and she suddenly felt tired, and none of this felt even remotely funny anymore. She'd almost been hit by a car. And the one person she thought might actually care didn't care at all.

And much as it killed her to admit, there was simply nothing she could do about that.

Chapter Thirteen

By Friday evening, the island of the Donovans' kitchen was covered in casseroles, trays of brownies, stacks of cookies, and muffins. Flowers of every color and shape filled every vase and jug and jar that Chip had collected over the years. The freezer was stacked with lasagna, more casseroles, and, of course, the cakes that Evie and Liam had baked together.

Had that just been a couple days ago? It felt like weeks, months! For the second time in just a short time, Evie was reminded of how quickly life could change.

"Someone brought over a couple bottles of wine," Abby called out from the kitchen to Evie, who was sitting in the living room, surrounded by her sister and cousins.

"Bring them in!" Margo called.

Hannah flashed a wicked grin. "I'll get the glasses."

Evie sighed. She was happy that her father had agreed, however reluctantly, to go into work tonight. It wouldn't do any of them any good to have him here, fretting over her. She was fine. Her injuries were minor, and they were healing. She wasn't in pain. Well, aside from the pain in her chest. Her heart hurt. It was a feeling she hadn't experienced before Liam came into her life. A phenomenon that made no sense to her until now. Heartbreak. She'd felt sadness over the years, disappointment and anger. But this? This was different. It was the pain of loss. Emotion manifested into physical pain.

If it didn't suck so much she would have found it fascinating.

"Has Eddie had any more leads on the driver?" Bridget asked.

Evie shook her head. "As it turns out, the person who thought they saw the first three letters of the license plate had mistakenly given their own first three letters, and then, no matter how much they thought about it, couldn't remember the numbers they thought they saw." Evie probably would have laughed about this, even found *that* fascinating, but again…it sort of stank.

"I know Eddie's been trying to get support for traffic cameras on Main Street. Maybe after this, the town will push it through." Margo looked down at her phone, which was starting to vibrate on the coffee table. "Oh. This is him now. I'll go outside so you girls can chat."

Bridget gave Evie a sad smile when the room had

cleared out, enough to make Evie say, again, "I'm fine." But even though her voice her firm, she felt a little wobbly, and on the verge of tears.

It was the drugs. And lack of sleep. That had it to be it.

"You seem down," Bridget said. "And I'm not so sure it's because of the accident. This is about Liam, isn't it?"

Evie hesitated. She didn't want to talk about Liam. Didn't see a point. But Liam was also Bridget's husband's good friend. If Evie was going to talk to anyone about this, Bridget would be the one.

"He ended things," Evie said. "Again."

Bridget didn't look surprised, but rather disappointed as she let out a sigh. "Liam's been through a lot. I know that Jack hoped his moving to Oyster Bay would help."

"He told me about his wife," Evie said. She felt ashamed, feeling upset that Liam had blown her off, when he had suffered a loss so much greater than hers.

Bridget looked surprised. "He told you about Ellen? He doesn't usually tell anyone about Ellen."

Evie struggled not to be flattered, or to read into this, but it verified what she already knew. She and Liam had a connection. Why end it?

"I guess he's not over her," she decided.

"Not over her death," Bridget clarified. "He won't stop blaming himself, no matter what anyone tells him."

"Blaming himself?" Evie felt her heart skip a beat. Something about this felt familiar. Strangely familiar. A man who had lost his wife. Who blamed himself for it.

Surely Liam wouldn't have written her a letter? Would he have?

"Oh, I shouldn't have said anything. I assumed he told you." Bridget looked distressed. "It was a car accident. I guess the roads were bad and Liam missed an exit and they were lost, somewhere with bad reception. He tried to reach for a map in the backseat and asked Ellen to do it instead. She took off her seatbelt so she could grab it and then Liam still tried and he took his eyes off the road."

"That's terrible!" Evie blinked hard, trying to push aside the images that were forming in her mind. But it was there, clear as the sky outside the French doors that led out to the back deck. She could see it, Liam, in the car, and the accident. The guilt.

What did that letter from that man say again? *I keep thinking that if I could turn back time, make a different decision, that she would still be here.*

It was Liam. She was sure of it.

"He's never gotten it over it, I'm afraid," Bridget said, shaking her head sadly. "The truck that hit them was at fault, actually. The driver was under the influence. Liam and Ellen, they probably didn't stand a chance. But try telling Liam that."

"Survivor's guilt," Evie said, thinking hard. He'd told her to get the map. She'd popped her seatbelt. A series of events that led to a disastrous outcome.

The letter! *If I'd made a different choice that day, maybe I'd be the one who died, not her.*

It *was* him. She was sure of it. And the more she

thought about it, the more she longed to go back, read the letter, make sure she'd said all the right things.

"What?" Bridget said.

"He feels bad that he lived and she didn't. He doesn't understand why he was given a second chance."

"Well, he's not making much of it," Bridget said. She tipped her head, giving Evie a sad look. "I'm sorry, Evie. If it helps at all, I think he did care for you. Jack said it was the most he's seen Liam move on since the accident."

Evie tried to find comfort in that but struggled. It didn't change the outcome. Liam was gone. Their relationship, or any hope for one, was over. Again.

"Did I miss anything?" Abby asked, coming back into the room with two bottles of wine and Hannah trailing, holding five wine glasses in her hand the way only a woman who had grown up in the restaurant business could master.

"I have some news," Margo said from the doorway. She looked somber, but there was a fire in her eyes when she looked at Evie. "Eddie said they were able to track down the car. They know who the driver was."

"Who?" everyone said at once. Everyone except Evie. Oyster Bay was a small town. She wasn't so sure she wanted to know. And from the look on Margo's face, it hadn't been a tourist in town for Fall Fest weekend.

"It was Wally Jennings. He blew through the light. He didn't even realize what he'd done when they questioned him. He didn't even remember being out for a drive that day at all. It was only when Martha said that she'd asked him to go into town for milk that he realized."

"His daughter wrote me a letter. To my column. She didn't identify herself, but it was obvious." Evie looked from her cousins to her sister, searching for an answer that she herself didn't have. "He's sick. This wasn't intentional."

"It doesn't mean that he didn't hurt somebody. You could have been killed!" Hannah's voice was shrill.

Evie glanced at Bridget, and right then, she understood. A split second. Everything could change. Just like it had for Liam.

"And now Wally is going to jail? That doesn't sit right either." Evie shook her head, replaying the letters. "Courtney had reached out to me. She was worried. He was forgetting things. He wasn't doing well. She didn't want him to drive. I…I should have agreed with her. Instead I advised her to tread carefully, defer to her mother." She looked up at her cousins and sister. "What if a child had been in that street instead of me?"

"You can't blame yourself, Evie," Hannah said firmly.

"I feel like I've failed at the one thing I've wanted to do." Maybe the hospital in Boston was right. Maybe she didn't understand people at all. Sure, she was book smart, but she'd kept to herself studying, instead of joining in.

"You're good at helping other people," Hannah said. "You always have been."

"But I can't help myself," Evie said. Her life was a mess. They all knew it, even if they didn't want to say it.

Hannah sighed. "It's easier to look at life from an outside point of view. It's easy to see what someone should say and do, when it's not you."

"Maybe, or maybe I know deep down what I would say to myself, but I've chosen to ignore my own advice. I'm my own worst enemy."

"What would you tell yourself to do?"

"A few things," Evie said. Too numerous to list. She wouldn't have gotten involved with Liam again, not when the warning signs were there, not when she knew that he was keeping something, putting up walls. And she wouldn't have been so hard on Hannah, either, not when all she ever wanted was to connect with their mother, and their sister.

Kelly. Evie thought of the unanswered letter waiting upstairs for her. She thought of her sister, waiting for a response. And she thought of what she would tell herself if the tables were turned. She would ask why. Why wouldn't she open the letter? What was she afraid of? What was she hiding from?

Connection? Rejection?

She stood, wincing slightly when she put her weight on her bad ankle.

"Where are you going?" Abby asked in alarm as Evie reached for her crutches and limped toward the hallway.

"I have a phone call to make," Evie said, glancing back at Hannah, whose smile was all the blessing she needed.

*

It had been over three weeks since she'd sent Evie that letter, but for some reason Kelly still checked the mailbox every day. She was back at the gym, holding her chin high when she passed Brian and Shannon on her way to the dance studio. She'd given up yoga. It reminded her too much of Chaz and her mother. She had expected to be told that she was avoiding things that brought her joy just to avoid the distress, but instead, in her last response from Ask Evie, which she had indeed read, she had been told that not being a masochist was equally important. And really, didn't she have enough going on right now?

But even though her sister had responded, professionally, to the two letters that Kelly had sent, she was yet to reply to the real one. It hurt Kelly to think about, and the knitting did help, just as Evie had promised it would. She spent most of her days with a ball of yarn in her lap now, instead of a bowl of ice cream. She'd moved on from scarves to cowls. With each stitch her mood did seem to lighten, the troubles seemed to fade, and the urgency to deal with them, or hide from them, or confront them, or even cry about them, well, it was delayed.

Tonight she planned to tackle hats. She'd been up until two finishing her cowl and she needed something to match it.

But first, she had to meet her mother. For their once monthly dinners.

They were meeting in China Town for dim sum and it

was Kelly who had suggested they meet at five so she could be at the yarn shop by six thirty. It was good to have a purpose again, a schedule. And an excuse to cut the meal short, if need be.

Anger festered and popped within her every time she thought of her mother and Chaz, in all his spandex glory. How long had it been going on? A week? A month? A year? Had he been ogling her while she went into downward dog? Had he—God help her—positioned her? These were the details she didn't know and really didn't want to know.

Her mother was already seated when Kelly arrived, five minutes late because she'd walked to try to calm herself down, and because, of course, she was still unemployed.

"Sorry I'm late," she said as she pulled out her chair. Apologizing! What was she apologizing for? If anyone should be apologizing it should be Loraine. For cheating on her father. For doing it in a public place. For breaking up their family or maybe for never investing in it in the first place.

"Is everything okay?" Loraine asked, picking up on Kelly's mood.

Evie hadn't told her how to handle this question. Only that she should remember that the relationship between two people was special to them, and that what Loraine and her father had was separate from her part in it. It was its own living thing. And maybe it had died. But that didn't mean that what she had with Loraine should die too.

Evie also said that it might take some time to understand that. Kelly wondered if Evie was speaking from experience. After all, Hannah had made it clear that Evie didn't support her decision to move west all those years ago.

She frowned. Of course Evie wouldn't ever reach out to her. She was the Chaz in this situation, wasn't she? Only, not really. Not if Evie was being fair. After all, she hadn't split up Evie's parents.

Her father had, she realized.

"No, everything is not okay," she said, because she couldn't hold it in any longer. So much was wrong. Brian. Shannon. Evie not wanting to have a relationship with her. Losing her job. If she'd had her knitting needles she might have taken out her frustration on the yarn, calmed herself down, and bought a little time. But the entire walk here she'd been arguing with her mother in her head. It had to be said. "I saw you. At Jolene's. Last weekend. With *Chaz*."

Her mother's expression remained flat. She didn't even twitch. After a long pause, during which Kelly nearly regretted saying anything and started wondering if she'd imagined everything, her mother said, "I didn't mean for you to see that."

So there it was. She hadn't denied it at all. And a part of Kelly thought she would.

Kelly didn't know whether this made her angrier or not. Yes, angrier, she decided, as her jaw clenched until her teeth started to hurt. She was very angry.

"And what about Dad?" she demanded.

"There are things about your father and me that you don't need to understand," Loraine said, reaching for her water.

Kelly stared at the water glass, wanting to knock it out of her mother's hand. How could she be thirsty at a time like this? She had just admitted to having an affair, to cheating.

"Your father has his life and I have mine," Loraine continued.

"You mean he *knows*?" This was a scenario that Kelly had never entertained. Sure, her dad traveled—a lot—and Loraine had her yoga and her meditation circle and her organic cooking club, but lots of couples had separate interests.

"Relationships are complicated, Kelly." Loraine sighed, and leaned back in her chair while the waitress brought them a bread basket. Kelly stared at it for a moment, knowing Loraine wouldn't touch it and would probably pull a face if Kelly did. Kelly narrowed her eyes, reached for the bleached white roll that was said to give cellulite, and buttered it, thickly. Loraine watched carefully, and finally said, "I'm not proud."

Kelly faltered. She hadn't expected that either. She waited, wondering what to say to that. She remembered what Evie had said, in her article. Her mother, Evie had said, was human. She wasn't just her mother, but she was also a woman, with toils and troubles just like everyone else.

Did Evie really believe that? Or did she just think that to make herself feel better, to rationalize what Loraine had done to her and Hannah? Or did she make no connection at all? Maybe Kelly was reading into things, wishing for things that weren't there. After all, Evie had never known whom she was writing to, had she?

She wanted to reply and ask what Evie thought about *her* mother, *their* mother, but she couldn't, not without giving herself away. So instead she read it again, and again, and she thought about it while she stitched and knitted and looped her fingers through the yarn, her projects growing larger in her lap with each row, the weight of it was satisfying.

Now, looking at her mother, she tried to see past the perfectly coiffed hair and the expertly applied makeup, with the fuchsia lip stick, and for the first time in her entire life, instead of feeling angry or sad or disappointed in Loraine, she almost felt sorry for her.

Loraine was restless and unsatisfied. She had spent her entire life looking for something and she clearly still hadn't found it. She was unhappy, Kelly realized. Whereas Kelly, aside from the whole Brian fiasco, well, Kelly couldn't exactly say she was unhappy at all.

"Where did you get that scarf?" her mother asked, peering at her.

Kelly sighed, waiting for the criticism. "I made it." She shoved the bread into her mouth. Let Loraine hit her with it all at once.

"You should consider selling those," Loraine said, surprising her.

"Sell them?"

"I mean it," Loraine said. She looked at the bread basket for a moment and muttered something to herself before reaching for a roll (whole wheat, but still).

Kelly felt a smile creep up her face as she touched the fabric gathered at her neck. Sell them? She considered it for a moment, wanting to hate the idea, but instead realizing it might just be the best piece of advice her mother had ever given her.

She left the restaurant that night feeling like it was, ironically, the nicest dinner she'd had with her mother in as long as she could remember. She smiled as she walked back to her neighborhood, deciding to go the yarn shop in the morning instead, her calves burning from the final hill, and when she got to her mailbox, this time she didn't even bother to check it.

She was good, she thought. Or at least, she would be. Someday.

With that, she reached for the door to the stairwell.

And then...the phone rang.

Chapter Fourteen

Against everyone's protests, Evie was determined to attend Fall Fest the next day. "And I'll be going back to work on Monday," she informed her father and sister hotly, glancing away from the knowing look in Hannah's eyes.

She'd made the decision last night, after an hour-long phone call with Kelly, which was surprisingly not awkward at all, and which left her beaming and full of hope. Despite her fears of engaging with Kelly, thanks to her column, she already had, and she already knew her a bit too, knew things that even Hannah didn't know yet. Things that made her feel bonded. Things that made her feel like this was actually her sister too.

It was time to start helping herself, to start taking her

own advice. Time to stop hiding from the hard stuff and deal with it instead.

And so, with Chip and Hannah's assistance, she frosted and finished the six cakes, and set them each in an open box to be transported to the trunk of her dad's car, where hopefully they wouldn't slide around too much.

"Drive slowly," she warned her dad.

Chip barked out a laugh that held no amusement. "Are you kidding me? I'll never drive so much as five miles over the speed limit in my life!"

"You're sure that you don't want to press charges?" Hannah asked once they were settled into the car, Evie in front, Hannah taking the backseat, along with Evie's crutches.

Evie had reached that decision last night too, only she didn't need time to think about it. "Wally Jennings has dementia, and his entire family is struggling with this. He's already being charged with speeding, running a red light, and a few other things. There's no need to punish him further."

Hannah didn't look convinced, but said nothing more on the subject. The ride into town was quick, and the leaves were starting to peak: colorful bursts of crimson, gold, and bright orange. Pumpkins hugged doorsteps, wreaths hung from doors. Normally, the change of season cheered her, but not today. Now it felt like a reminder that time was passing and that her life was just as unsettled as it had been last spring.

The Fall Fest was already crowded, even at only ten in the morning, and Evie recognized the worry that creased her father's brow—and the way he tried to hide it.

"You go to the food stand," Evie said. It was custom for The Lantern to host a stand at the event, along with other local vendors. It was tradition that Chip served lobster rolls, fish and chips, and cider. Hard cider. Needless to say, it was usually the most popular spot in the town square, unless you factored in Angie's cider donuts.

"Not until I've carried these in for you." Chips popped the trunk of the car.

"I can do it," Hannah said. When Chip started to protest, she said, "Now no more excuses!"

Chip grinned. "What would I do without you girls?"

"Fortunately, that's something you don't have to think about," Hannah said, but Evie knew what they were all thinking. What Chip had thought about. First when Hannah left town for all those years and more recently Evie's accident.

Evie waited until her father had disappeared from site before she propped the crutches against the side of the car and tried to put weight on her sprained ankle, but she knew it was no use.

"It's okay to let people help you, you know." Hannah lifted an eyebrow at Evie's obvious frustration.

"Are you trying to say that I can dish it out, but I can't take it?" Evie hobbled alongside Hannah over the uneven grass. The cake walk was set up at the far end of the town square, of course, near the pie baking contest.

"Hey, you said it, not me."

"Well, I'm working on that," Evie said. "I guess it's been easier thinking of other people's problems instead of my own."

"You can't hide forever," Hannah said.

"When did you become the wise older sister?" Evie joked, but she appreciated it, a lot. Hannah was walking briskly, no doubt eager to meet up with Dan and Lucy, and Evie was struggling to keep up. She scanned the festival, looking for Liam, knowing that she would have to face him eventually. She didn't plan to hide anymore. Didn't want to. Hiding didn't change anything. It just delayed the inevitable.

"I'm glad that you called Kelly last night," Hannah said as she set the cake down next to a truly exquisite towering chocolate creation that made Evie feel inadequate. She looked at her own effort, the layered strawberries and cream cake that was decorated simply, with sliced berries on top, and felt grateful that the cakes weren't being labeled.

"Tags!" Beverly Wright was holding a square of folded cardstock and a pen out to her. "We're tagging all the cakes this year, so everyone knows what they're receiving and, of course, who made it!" Her knowing smile turned a little smug as she set her card next to the chocolate tower, which must have been at least ten layers high, covered in ganache, and a mountain of chocolate curls.

Hannah rolled her eyes and walked off to get another cake. Evie fought off a sigh and picked up the pen. She hesitated as she brought it to the paper. It would be so much easier to write her own name, but that would be hiding again, wouldn't it? From the memories. From the heartache. From the truth.

Without considering it further, she wrote, "Evie Donovan and Liam Bauer" on the card and set it beside their entry.

Bev's eyes widened with interest. "Evie and *Liam*."

"That's right," Evie said simply. She glanced back at the car, wishing Hannah would hurry up, and knowing she was trapped. By the time she reached the car, Hannah would be back, and besides, these crutches were killing her armpits.

"I'd heard that the two of you had something going on this summer, but I just couldn't believe it." Bev's eyes roamed Evie's face, looking for confirmation. "Well, things aren't always as they seem, are they?"

Evie gave a small laugh, thinking just how true this was, and how often even she still failed to look beyond the surface. "No, Bev, they are definitely not always as they seem."

But sometimes, she thought, you had no choice but to accept them at face value.

*

Liam caught the time on the oven clock and cursed under his breath. Fall Fest had already started and he'd only finished one cake, instead of the planned three, and truth be told, he wasn't so sure it was even edible.

The doorbell rang as he quickly spread the last of the frosting on the top layer, realizing only now that he should have doubled the batch, maybe even tripled it, because it would never cover the sides, and weren't cakes usually frosted all the way around?

"It's open!" he called out, knowing it would be Jack because he'd called him last night and asked him to come over today.

"What the hell is going on here?" Jack asked from the kitchen doorway. "I mean, we've all been worried about you, dude, but now I'm beginning to think you're even worse off than we feared."

"Very funny," Liam said when Jack started to laugh. It was the first time they'd made light of his circumstances, and strangely, it didn't feel bad or wrong. It felt natural. It felt like a release.

Time had passed, he realized. Maybe there was hope for him yet.

"Don't tell me this is what I'm supposed to be picking up." Jack walked farther into the kitchen and inspected Liam's handiwork. "No offense, Liam, but don't quit your day job."

"I don't plan to," Liam said, even though that wasn't exactly true. After what happened this week, he did think about leaving the paper. About packing up his stuff, heading back to New York. It didn't take long to realize that he didn't want to go back. Or backwards. He didn't want to wander the streets, every corner a fresh memory. He wanted to make new memories.

But he didn't want to forget, either. That was the tricky part.

"I wasn't so sure," Jack said, giving him an appraising look. "Bridget told me that you broke things off with Evie."

Liam set the knife back in the bowl of frosting. It had a grainy texture that didn't seem like any of the frostings he'd ever had before, but it was too late to worry about it now.

"Evie could have been killed," Liam said.

"But she wasn't," Jack pointed out.

Liam shook his head. It wasn't that simple. "What happened on Thursday—"

Jack held up a hand, his expression softening. "I know. It reminded you of what happened with Ellen. But Evie isn't Ellen, Jack."

"No one is Ellen," Liam said. He loved her, he always would, but for the first time since she'd passed he'd realized he could love someone else, too, if he let himself.

"You can't control everything in life," Jack continued.

Liam nodded. He'd heard this a hundred times over the years, but it didn't bring him any comfort. Life was unpredictable. It could change in an instant. How could anyone take comfort in that?

"I shouldn't have called out to her," Liam said, finally verbalizing the one, horrible thought that he couldn't shake. "If I hadn't, she might have crossed the street before the car came."

"You saved her," Jack said firmly. "If she hadn't seen the panic in your face, she wouldn't have turned around and seen the car at all. She got out of the way in time because of you."

Liam pulled in a breath, processing this theory. It was possible, he supposed. Still, he couldn't quite accept the order of events.

"You have to stop blaming yourself, Liam. What happened to Ellen...the truck was at fault. Ellen chose to pop the seatbelt for a minute. Things happen. Terrible things happen. You can let them define you, and control you, or you can take a chance."

Liam looked down at his cake, at the sad offering he'd made for the cake walk, replaying that night in Evie's kitchen. He'd been happy that night. Genuinely happy. And since then, he'd been miserable.

"Maybe I'll bring this over to the festival then," he said.

Jack grinned. "Good. Cause don't for a minute think that I was going to be seen carrying it!"

Liam laughed and slapped his friend on the back on the way out the door, nearly dropping the cake, that now seemed to be deflating before his eyes until he worried the top layer would slip off.

"You know you're welcome to join Bridget and Emma and me," Jack said, but Liam shook his head.

"There's someone else I need to see." If she'd even talk to him.

*

Evie strolled the grounds of the town green, or hobbled, she should say. She returned the smiles of those who gave them, many people stopping to ask how she was doing, or exclaim their distress that Wally Jennings of all people was responsible.

He wasn't at the event. If he had been, Evie would have liked to have spoken with him. Or Martha. Or even Courtney. She'd reach out to them next week, she decided. No doubt her sister wouldn't approve, but Evie was in the mood to practice forgiveness.

She'd forgiven her mother a long time ago for walking out on them. It was the only way to find peace and move on. And last night, she'd forgiven herself for not reaching out to Kelly sooner. Life was too short to hold grudges or cling to negative feelings.

But when she turned back toward the cake walk, eager for a bench to sit on, and saw Liam, all those good feelings seemed to disappear.

He'd come. She really didn't think he would. Maybe he had assumed she wouldn't be here. That he wouldn't have to worry about explaining himself. Or maybe...

He was facing her now. Staring at her with a look of purpose mixed with apprehension. She waited a beat, to see if he'd turn around, set down the cake and walk off, but he didn't move at all. He just stood there, holding the ugliest cake Evie had ever seen in her life.

And despite herself, she burst out laughing. She laughed and laughed, and then, for some horrible, humiliating reason, she started to cry, and she couldn't stop.

"Evie?" Damn it, it was him. She was staring at the ground, but she knew that voice, sensed his presence, felt his heat as he stood close.

"It's the damn pain killers," she sniffed. "Don't mind me."

"You've had a rough couple of days," he said, and she dared to look up at him, into his warm eyes, that crinkled at the corners with concern.

Well, she didn't need his pity.

"I'm afraid I didn't do anything but add to them," he said.

Evie narrowed her eyes as her tears seemed to immediately dry up. "Don't flatter yourself," she said.

She was crossing a line, perhaps. After all, the man was still technically her boss. But not for long. Monday would be her last day. She'd set up a blog, help people that way, while she job searched for something more permanent.

She might have told a patient that they were hiding by doing this, the way she'd told Kelly (she still couldn't believe that it had been Kelly who had been writing to her!) that she shouldn't avoid the gym. But she'd also told Kelly not to be a masochist, and really, there was only so much that Evie could take. She was human. Just like all her patients. Just like the members of this community.

Just like Liam, she thought, softening a bit.

But only a bit.

Liam set his cake down on the table, next to the lemon chiffon entry she'd finished this morning. He frowned as he looked at the card, and then picked it up. "Evie and Liam," he read. He looked at her sidelong, giving a slow smile. "Has a nice ring to it."

Evie firmed her mouth. She wouldn't be feeding into that statement, even if it was true.

"As you said, it's been a long week," she said, eager to get away. But this time, she couldn't run off, even if she wanted to. She shifted her weight on her crutches, feeling uncomfortable.

Sensing it, Liam jutted his chin to a nearby bench and held out a hand. "Heading that way?"

She nodded, all too aware as she allowed him to help her over to the bench that this was just like the first time they'd met, when the blisters from her shoes had made walking so painful she had nearly tripped on her way to a chair at Bridget's rehearsal dinner. And there was a hand, sure and steady, holding her up.

If she could go back to that night, would she have done it all differently? Worn sensible shoes, made it to the corner to sit comfortably by herself, having no idea that she was sparing herself all this heartache?

Or that she was missing out on this feeling of being alive?

"Thank you," she said, as she finally reached the

bench. She hoped that would be the end of it, that he would go, and that she wouldn't have to see him again until she gave her notice Monday morning. It would be for two weeks, of course. She may have changed over the past few months, but she hadn't changed *that* much.

"I should have called," Liam said suddenly.

She looked up at him, holding his gaze. "Yes. You should have."

"My wife, she died in a car accident. And what happened on Thursday, it brought up a lot of bad memories." His jaw seemed to twitch. "I kept thinking what it would have felt like if I lost you."

"But you lost me anyway," she said. "You pushed me away."

"I thought it would be easier that way," he said, dropping to sit beside her. "But..."

There was a long pause. Evie watched him, hunched over, resting his elbows on his knees, looking at everything but her. "But?"

Finally, he turned to her, giving a soft smile that made her heart sing in a way she had hoped that it wouldn't anymore. "I liked myself better when I was with you. I liked...life better when I was with you. I guess I didn't want to think about not having you in my life."

"But that's exactly what you did," she pointed out. "You cut me out."

"Maybe it was easier to do it first. To be in control this time. To have life on my terms."

She smiled. "There are some things in life you can't control, I've learned. Other people." She was thinking of her mother, maybe. And Liam. And Wally, who had plowed through that intersection. The truck driver, who had killed Ellen. And maybe, she was thinking of herself. She wasn't as predictable as she'd once been, after all.

"I know I've messed this up," Liam said turning to face her, really face her, until she was forced to look up, confront the matter, and make a decision. "But this…this isn't something I want to end."

She was breathing heavily, and normally this sort of conversation would have made her start to itch, make the hives start to spread and the panic start to rise and then she'd run, hide, open a book, and stay in her shell, where she was nice and safe and…alone.

"I understand more than you think," she said. "We have a lot in common."

He sat a little straighter. "Does this mean I get a second chance?"

She raised an eyebrow at him, but she was teasing and he knew it. "I think it's actually a third chance, but who's counting?"

"I am," he said, reaching out to take her hand. "Two weeks for the first chance. Two weeks for the second. And all the time in the world for the third."

"I like the sound of that," she said, leaning in to kiss him just long enough for Bev Wright to let out a gasp so loud that all Evie could do was smile.

Epilogue

It was tradition for Thanksgiving to be spent at Mimi's house. The seafront Victorian mansion was more than large enough to house the Harper family and, by extension, the Donovans. But now the Harper family had grown. Margo had Eddie, Bridget had Jack and little Emma, of course, and Abby was happily reunited with Zach. Even Mimi herself was remarried, settled down in Serenity Hills with Earl. And the house, much as it would always be a family house, meant to be passed along through the generations that would be born and raised in Oyster Bay, was a public house now, and the inn didn't close for holidays.

Besides, Chip was eager to put his shiny new kitchen to use.

"You know, Dad, the guest list is pretty big this year,"

Hannah said After all, she had not just Dan but his daughter Lucy in her life now. "Even Evie has a guest this year."

"I heard that!" Evie said, giving her sister a rueful smile as she walked into the kitchen, wearing a new, sweater dress for the occasion. "I think what Hannah is trying to say is that it might be your turn now."

They'd never broached the topic; the mere idea of their father dating anyone had come and gone over the years. But it saddened Evie to think that her father might be feeling lonely, especially since Hannah had moved out two weeks ago and Evie's boxes were ready to go into her new apartment off Main Street. A far cry from her city life in Boston, but a pleasant change all the same.

"Don't go trying to set me up," Chip said as he checked on the turkey. He closed the oven door and turned to them. "Everything happens on its own time."

True, Evie thought. The doorbell rang and Evie walked to the hall, expecting it to be Abby, who had promised to stop by early to get her sweet potato casserole in the oven. Instead, Evie was surprised to see Sarah standing on the front stoop. She all but thrust the pecan pie into Evie's arms and said, "I need to tell you something before Liam gets here."

Uh-oh. Evie didn't like the sound of that, and she quickly pulled Sarah inside, bringing a few rustling leaves in with her. Her heart was pounding as she stared at her friend. "What is it?"

She knew it wouldn't be something to do with her. She

and Liam had talked enough now for her to know that once Liam had decided to commit to this, he was all in, one hundred percent. But something in Sarah's eyes worried her. *Please don't say you still have a crush*, she thought miserably.

"I'm going to give my notice at the paper tomorrow," Sarah whispered.

Evie blinked. She hadn't expected that one. "Where are you going? You're not leaving Oyster Bay, are you?"

"No, nothing like that." Sarah's blue eyes sparkled. "I'm going to join Melanie and Chloe at Bayside Brides. They want to expand the business. And well, you know how much I love weddings and wedding dresses and all that!"

Evie gave a small smile. Yes, she did know. The whole town knew. "Well, I'm happy for you. And a bit relieved, too."

"Relieved?" Now Sarah frowned.

Evie winced. "Well, back when Liam came to the paper I know that you were interested…"

Sarah stared at her for a moment and then burst out laughing. "I was never interested. I wanted to see if *you* were interested. And no better way to find out than to see how you'd feel if another girl were to move in on your guy."

Evie felt her jaw slack. "You mean, you were just trying to get me to open up?"

Sarah patted her arm. "You can be far too private for

your own good, Evie. And yes, jealousy was my tactic, you might say."

Evie started laughing, but she still couldn't quite believe she hadn't figured that out. "Well, it worked."

"Might be worth trying on your patients!" Sarah grinned, but then leaned in when the doorbell rang. "Remember, not a word to Liam. I want to tell him in person tomorrow."

"Of course," Evie said, sidestepping her to open the door. Liam stood on the front step, looking particularly handsome in his brown jacket and plaid scarf.

"Come outside for a moment," he said, when he spotted Sarah. "I have something I want to tell you before everyone arrives."

This day was getting weirder and weirder and the party hadn't even started yet, Evie thought, as she matched Sarah's puzzled expression and stepped outside into the smoky autumn air. Her heart was pounding, she realized, and she wasn't sure why. After all, today was a good day, a wonderful day, really, a day when everyone she loved would be here inside her house. Liam included, she realized.

"I got a call yesterday. From New York." Liam's eyes were full of light and anticipation when she looked up at him, her heart sinking.

"New York?" She knew what this meant, and why hadn't she considered it? Wouldn't Liam eventually be drawn back, be offered bigger and better opportunities?

He nodded. "I didn't want to tell you because I wasn't

sure what would happen."

Evie stifled a groan. So much for a wonderful first holiday together. She had let her guard down, stopped thinking with her head, stopped bracing herself for worst case scenarios. She'd fallen, started living every day with her heart and now, well, it had caught up with her.

"I talked to some of the people I used to know. People in the media."

Evie frowned. "Media?"

"I talked to them about your column. And yesterday evening I got a call." His grin broadened. "What do you think about being syndicated?"

Evie blinked. She was waiting for him to tell her that he was going back to New York, trying to decide if she would go too, or if she would stay, and now, he was saying something else entirely different? "So you're telling me you're not going back to New York." She needed to be sure she was hearing this correctly.

"What?" He squinted at her, and then grabbed her hands. "I'm telling you that people love your column. They want to grow it. Don't you see what this means, Evie?"

Her mind was spinning but on some level she did know what this would mean. It meant that somehow, some way, it had all worked out. All those years studying, skipping the prom to cram for finals, working for one goal had finally paid off. Only not in the way she had expected. But better. So much better.

"It's like it was meant to be," she said, chewing on this thought for a moment. Since when did she believe in such nonsense?

Since Liam, she thought, looking up at him with a heart so full, she thought it would burst.

"I only wish I'd been the one who discovered you," Liam said ruefully.

She grinned. "You did. Just in a different way."

"A less…professional way?"

"Does this mean you won't be my boss anymore?" she asked, thinking that she would rather miss not seeing him at the office every day.

"Afraid so," he said. "But that's probably for the best. A little too complicated, wouldn't you say?"

"I happen to like complicated," Evie said, as two cars pulled into her driveway and her cousins began to pour out. She sighed, looking up at Liam. "Looks like we'll have to save this conversation for another time."

"We have all the time in the world," Liam said, as he took her hand and followed her into the house.

OLIVIA MILES writes feel-good women's fiction and heartwarming contemporary romance that is best known for her quirky side characters and charming small town settings. She lives just outside Chicago with her husband, young daughter, and two ridiculously pampered pups.

Olivia loves connecting with readers. Please visit her website at www.OliviaMilesBooks.com to learn more.